AUTHOR'S N

This novel is one of those which first appeared under the pen-name of Emma Woodhouse previously only available in paperback. In re-issuing them in a hardback edition for the first time and under my own name, Severn House have asked me to explain how they came to be written.

From earliest childhood I was always a compulsive writer, though of course I had no idea then that I would ever be able to earn my living by writing. I completed my first full-length children's novel at the age of ten – a harrowing tale of a misunderstood orphan and an untamed pony – and over the next eight years I wrote eight more, but though I regularly sent them off to publishers, none was ever accepted for publication.

At the age of eighteen I went off to university in Scotland, and there wrote my first adult novel. I submitted it to a publisher, but it was rejected, though with a kind and encouraging note that I should keep trying. I had no need of that particular advice – I had already begun a second novel, THE WAITING GAME. It took me some time to complete, but when at last I submitted it for a competition for unpublished writers, my persistence was rewarded: THE WAITING GAME won the 1972 NEL Young Writer's Award.

NEL also took my next novel, SHADOWS ON THE MOUNTAIN; and then another publisher approached me with a commission to write three romances. In those days, publishers believed that a writer had to have a different name for each separate kind of book they wrote, and since the romances would be quite different from my previous two novels, I was asked to choose a pseudonym. At the time I was in the middle of my annual re-reading of the Jane Austen novels, and happened to have got up to *Emma*, so I suggested Emma Woodhouse as a pen-name.

Thus I embarked on my first three commissioned books; but meanwhile I had to earn a living. My husband at that time was at college and not earning, so I was doing a part-time evening job as well as my daytime office job to make ends meet. Add to that the running of a home, and the social life of a newly-married couple, and it didn't leave much time for writing; but when you accept a commission, it is vital that you hand in the work on time. Every spare moment of evenings and weekends found me pounding away at the typewriter. Somehow I did it: the books were delivered by the deadline; and in giving satisfaction in this first contract I paved the way for what was to be my career as a full-time novelist.

As I write this, more than thirty books later, my novel EMILY has just won the RNA Novel of the Year Award for 1993; but in spite of all the recent excitements, I still have a particular fondness for my Emma Woodhouse books. They remind me of those struggling days, and I contemplate with amazement the youthful energy that was needed to produce them while juggling with so many other balls in the air. I am very glad to see them reissued in this handsome Severn House edition, with my own name on the cover, and I hope you will enjoy reading them as much as I enjoyed writing them.

A RAINBOW SUMMER

Cynthia Harrod-Eagles

SEVERN SH HOUSE

This first hardcover edition published in Great Britain 1994 by
SEVERN HOUSE PUBLISHERS LTD of
9–15 High Street, Sutton, Surrey SM1 1DF.
Previously published in 1976 in paperback format only
under the pseudonym of *Emma Woodhouse*.
This edition complete with new introduction from the author.

British Library Cataloguing in Publication Data
Harrod-Eagles, Cynthia
  Rainbow Summer. – 2Rev. ed
  I. Title
  823.914 [F]

  ISBN 0-7278-4611-6

Typeset by Hewer Text Composition Services, Edinburgh.
Printed and bound in Great Britain by
Redwood Books, Trowbridge, Wiltshire.

CHAPTER ONE

It had been a wet July, and it looked like being a wet August too. Janet leaned her chin on her fist and stared out of the window in her corner of the office, and felt how dull everything was. The sky was leaden, and the rain fell in a warm, steady drizzle, blackening the dirty brick of the building opposite, gathering at the top of the window-frame and running down in fat, greasy drops, leaving cleaner trails through the gathered soot on the glass, like tear marks down a child's dirty face.

The wet streets were empty, except for the occasional passing of cars, swishing through the puddles and occasionally skidding a little when they tried to race the traffic lights at the end of the street and didn't make it. A wet August was enough to depress a saint; and to make it worse, she had taken her holidays in June, so she had nothing to look forward to until Christmas, when, knowing *this* firm, they would only get the bare minimum two days off anyway. And that was – still another four and a half months away. Four and a half months in this place, with no excitement, nothing to make one week different from another. I shall go screaming mad, she thought.

She glanced up at the clock – nearly eleven, thank God. The coffee would be coming round any minute. She studied her hands gloomily. The nails needed attention, and the nail on the third finger of the left hand was broken. That was this firm again! Filing cabinets that broke your fingernails, chairs that ripped your tights, waste-paper bins that took the skin off your shins. And pens – she let out a sound of exasperation as she looked more closely at the hand that held the office-issue ballpoint – pens that leaked sticky ink all over you, ink that wouldn't come out no matter how often you washed your blouses.

'What was that word you just said, Janet Anderson?' a voice said in mock horror. That was Vicky walking past with a pile of bulging files to go back in the filing cabinet. Janet smiled up at her. Vicky was a madcap, a tearaway; she wore the weirdest clothes, never seeming to mind what she looked like. Her nails were bitten, her stockings usually had holes in them, and her hair was a tangled bird's nest that changed colour almost weekly; but she was good fun, and never minded what she said, even to the managers. 'I'll report you to Mr. Tomlinson, if I hear any more o' that carry-on,' Vicky said, and trying to wag a finger at Janet she let the top two files slip off the pile, and they fell, scattering papers over the floor. 'Oh, sod it!' she exclaimed, and Janet started to laugh.

'Here, I'll give you a hand,' Janet said, and got down on her knees beside the other girl to retrieve the papers.

'Oh, just stuff 'em in any old how. We'll not be lookin' at this one for another six months,' Vicky said, crumpling up the letters and documents and thrusting them back inside the covers. 'Beats me why they keep all this old stuff – no-one ever wants any of it again.'

'Efficiency, Miss Duke, efficiency,' Janet said pompously.

'Ey-up, talking of penguins, here comes Spotty now,' Vicky said under her breath, and pushing the last piece of paper into the file she put it back on the pile and stood up, just as 'Spotty' Tomlinson came out of his office at the end of the room. Janet sat down hastily in her seat and pretended to blow her nose to hide her laughter as Tomlinson came up the gangway between the rows of desks towards them.

He was only about twenty-eight or -nine, but by his manner he could have been forty. He was short and thin, with wispy, sandy hair that did not cover the pink scalp on the top, and had a distressing tendency to spots that would have made Janet feel sorry for him, if he had not tried to compensate for his lack of personal attraction by being as objectionable as possible to everyone. Vicky called him Spotty or The Penguin, and could do a fair imitation of his pompous, strutting walk; but he was all-powerful in the sales department of Emerson's Electrical, and nearly everyone else was afraid of him.

He paused in front of the two girls now and frowned at them. 'There doesn't seem to be much work going on here, judging by the noise,' he said. 'You girls aren't here to lark about,

6

you know. If you haven't got enough to do, I can always find you something.'

'It's eleven o'clock, Mr. Tomlinson,' said Vicky perkily. 'Time for a cup o' coffee and a Penguin.'

Janet gave a snort of helpless laughter into her handkerchief, and Tomlinson's frown intensified.

'What's the matter with you?' he demanded.

'She swallowed the wrong way, she'll be all right in a moment, won't you love?' Vicky said sympathetically, and under cover of patting Janet's shoulder gave her a sharp pinch that went a long way to sobering her up. 'Oh look, here's the tea lady, Mr. Tomlinson, sir. Have I to bring your cup into your office for you?'

'No, I'll have mine later,' he said, and giving them a last doubtful scowl he went on his way.

'Thanks, Vicky. I just couldn't stop laughing,' Janet said when he had gone.

'You'll get yourself the sack if you carry on like that, my girl,' Vicky said with an air of age and wisdom. 'Here, I'll just dump these files, and I'll come over and have my coffee with you.'

Two minutes later Vicky was perched on the edge of Janet's desk and the girls had their cups of coffee in front of them and lighted cigarettes in their hands.

'I don't think I'd much mind if I did get the sack,' Janet said, with another glance out of the window at the rain.

'I know what you mean,' Vicky sighed. 'What with Spotty prancing around like a little bald Hitler, and Mrs. Landon making eyes at the reps, for all she could be their mother – it's enough to drive anybody mad.'

'I don't mind Mrs. Landon,' Janet said. 'I feel rather sorry for her, really. It must be hard for her, being a widow, and bringing up all those children on her own – and she's quite young, really. She can't be more than about thirty-two.'

Vicky snorted with disparagement.

'I'll tell you what about our Merry Widow – I don't believe she's got any kids at all! Have you ever seen them? Have you ever seen photos of them? No – and neither has anyone else. She makes them up – they're her fantasy. The way the rest of

7

us dream of being abducted by Steve McQueen, she dreams of having four kids to belt around and tuck up in bed.'

Janet laughed.

'You go too far sometimes, Vicky. Why should anyone make up four children? Anyway, even if she does, that's all the more reason to be sorry for her.'

'All right then, Mrs. Florence Nightingale Freud, what d'you want to leave for, if you love everyone so much?'

'Oh, I don't know. I'm just fed up with everything. This office, this town. It's always raining, and there's never anything to do. I just want to see some new places and do something different – I just want a change.'

'Eh, you have got the blues, haven't you? Now, you just listen to your Aunty Vicky – what you need is a good night out, with a couple of fellas that are good for a laugh. I'll fix something up for you. Can't see an old pal in the dumps.'

'No, really,' Janet began, but Vicky overruled her.

'I'll get it all fixed up – leave it to me.'

Janet didn't think she'd enjoy an evening of Vicky's sort in the least, but she didn't protest any more. It was kind of Vicky, and maybe she wanted company. But even if she did enjoy it, it wasn't going to solve the problem of her 'blues' – that was something much more serious than just temporary boredom.

Mrs. Landon poked her head round the door of her office, which was just behind Janet's desk, and said,

'Janet, could you come in here for a minute, dear?'

'I'd better be on my way,' Vicky said. 'Save me a seat in t'canteen at lunchtime.' And she jumped off the desk and strutted off, whistling, while Janet smoothed down her skirt and went into the tiny office whose door was never closed. Mrs. Landon had no official title for her job, but while Mr. Tomlinson was called Sales Manager, and had the power of all punishment in the department, it was Mrs. Landon who seemed to do all the work, and it was to her that everyone went when they had a problem about their job or wanted to know anything about electrical goods. Everyone in the firm seemed to know where Mrs. Landon's office was, and no-one ever came out of there without the help they went in for.

8

Mrs. Landon looked up and smiled as Janet came in, and said in her pleasant southern voice, 'Would you mind going down to Mr. Waldron and asking him for the Manderville correspondence file? He borrowed it yesterday and forgot to give it back.'

'Yes, O.K.,' Janet said and was about to go when the older woman called her back.

'Oh, and Janet —'

'Yes?'

Mrs. Landon seemed to study her for a minute, then said gently, 'With the door being open, I hear a lot of things that I'm probably not meant to hear.' Janet blushed a little, thinking she was referring to what Vicky had said about the imaginary children, but she went on, 'When I was eighteen, I went away from this town, to London. I thought it would be the answer to all my dreams. It wasn't, and I came back eventually, not much better off than I went away.' She paused, looking into the distance as if she were choosing the right words to say. 'In a way, it isn't any of my business, but I hope you'll take what I say as kindly meant. What I want to say to you is that it can be a very good thing to get away to a new place, but don't go with too many high hopes, and above all, don't go unprepared. Make sure you've got somewhere to stay when you get there, and enough money for your ticket home if you don't like it.'

Janet nodded, and waited. The older woman smiled; she looked quite pretty when she smiled, and it seemed a waste that she should be a widow. Mrs Landon reached into a drawer in the desk at which she was sitting and took something out which she offered to Janet. Janet took it – it was a photograph of a younger, plumper Mrs. Landon holding a very new baby up to the camera and smiling; it was a peculiar smile, seeming to hold as much sorrow as it did pleasure. Janet looked at it for a long time, and felt her cheeks burning with embarrassment, but when she handed it back, Mrs. Landon was laughing.

'That's the youngest. Tell Vicky I can't produce concrete evidence, but they're all quite real. Off you go, then.'

Janet made her escape, and muttered to herself as she went

9

down the stairs to Advertising, 'I'll kill that Vicky. Poor Mrs. L.'

Mr. Waldron, the advertising under-manager, was the office heart-throb, and also something of an office wolf. Pauline, his secretary, called him 'Tall, Dark and Hands-off', and said that he was working his way round the building, for he had been out with her, with Vicky, who worked in Despatch, and with Vera from Admin. Pauline gave Janet a wink over the top of her typewriter as she came in and said, 'He's in there,' nodding towards the open door of his cubby-hole. 'I can bet what you've come for – Mrs. Landon wants to know if To-night's the Night. Tell her she can use the internal phone – he's had a scrambler-device fixed on his. We've had the Technical Department in all morning – can't have anything interfering with his love life, can we?'

'You are cruel,' Janet laughed.

'So's he – his meteoric passage through Emerson's is littered with broken hearts – mine included,' Pauline said, and she sighed sentimentally and laid a hand on her brow.

'Pauline!' a voice bellowed from the inner sanctum, 'have you phoned the *Evening Argus* yet?'

'Yes, darling,' Pauline trilled back.

'Don't call me darling,' the irascible voice bellowed back. 'Who are you talking to in there?'

Janet hastened to the door of his room.

'It's only me, Mr. Waldron.'

'Oh – Janet, come in. What can I do for you?' The bull changed to a dove, and Tom Waldron hastily rearranged his face and leaned back in his chair, the picture of the Young Executive. A very meaning cough from outside started a smile on Janet's face, which she tried to repress as she said, 'Mrs. Landon asked me to ask you for the correspondence file for Manderville's.'

'Oh yes, of course, certainly, I have it right here,' he said with a great show of efficiency, taking it out of his top drawer and handing it to her.

'Thank you,' Janet said, and turned to go.

'Er, Janet?'

'Yes?' Janet said, unencouragingly.

'I was wondering, er – I thought perhaps —'

'I've got Mr. Mayhew of the *Post* on the line for you, sir,' Pauline yelled at that moment, with a heavy emphasis on the 'sir'.

'Oh, all right,' Waldron said unwillingly, and Janet nipped out. Pauline dropped her another wink as she passed, and as Janet went out of the door, she heard Pauline shout, 'Oh dear, I seem to have lost him. Must've got cut off somehow. I'll ring him again.'

Laughing, Janet went back upstairs. Pauline certainly knew how to handle him. She wondered for a moment if it might have been fun to go out with Tom Waldron, but the very fact that she wondered told her that it wouldn't have. It was not a new boy-friend she needed. It suddenly struck her that what she really wanted was to be in love. She was twenty, and though she'd had several boy-friends, she'd never cared greatly for any of them. She envied other girls she knew who were or had been in love – their lives seemed much more special. Even Mrs. Landon had a special section of her memory that she could retreat to when life seemed too dull. But Janet despaired of ever meeting anyone she could fall in love with, even temporarily, in this town. There must be more to life than this!

At one o'clock Janet switched off her calculating machine, swept the invoices on her desk into a pile, put her leaky ball-point into her drawer, picked up her handbag and headed for the canteen. The queue was already out of the door and half way across the landing, but as she moved to join it she saw Vicky further up near the counter waving her arms about like a windmill, trying to catch her attention. Janet was hesitant to 'push in', but as she reached Vicky with all her doubt on her face, the latter pulled her into line and said cheerfully,

'Don't worry, love, I've told them behind I'm eatin' for two.'

'What's on the me-and-you today, then?' Janet asked, and the little plump girl, Nora, who worked with Vicky in Despatch, said, 'I don't think I'd better tell you, it might put you off.'

'Don't be soft,' Vicky said scornfully. 'You're talking to the

11

girl with the Iron Stomach.' She patted Janet on the shoulder with a proprietorial air. 'This girl is famous as being the only living soul ever to eat two portions of Emersons' Steak and Kidney Pie, and keep it down. That was a feat, only rivalled by Mr. Tomlinson's feet, two feet long in their bare shoes. I said to him, is that a foot, and he said, well I don't use it as a rule.'

'You know, I shall miss you when I leave,' Janet said, laughing.

'Leave, you're not leavin'?' Vicky sounded shocked. 'Who is it? Tell me his name, and I'll —' She bunched her fist threateningly, and looking round caught the eye of meek little Horace, the junior from the post room. She frowned at him severely, and he blenched. 'Have you been annoying Miss Anderson, Horace? Speak up now, tell the truth.'

'Oh, Vicky, stop, it isn't fair,' Janet said, giving her a shake. 'Listen, I've got something to tell you,' she went on, to distract Vicky's attention from the poor boy, who was going red. 'Mrs. Landon showed me a photo of her youngest baby, and said to tell you that they're all just as real.'

'Go on, she didn't!' Vicky's face was alight with astonished delight. 'She heard me then?'

'She hears everything. She never shuts her door, you know.'

'Well, if she never shuts her door, she deserves all she gets. People should have the decency to let other people gossip about them in peace. Still, I still don't believe she's got four kids. That could have been a photo of any baby, a nephew or niece or anything.'

'Well, she was holding it in the picture.'

'That doesn't mean anything.'

'You are sceptical. You should have seen the photo – the expression on her face. You'd have believed it then.'

'You're a soft devil,' Vicky said affectionately. 'You'd believe anything you were told rather than hurt a feeling.'

'You know what I heard about Mrs. L.,' Nora said, picking up a tray from the edge of the counter. 'I heard she was sweet on Tom Waldron, and keeps going down to his office to try and get him to ask her out.'

'That's silly,' Janet said. The more gossip she heard, the

12

fonder she felt of Mrs. Landon.

'Well, ever since he's joined the company, she's been wearing all her smartest clothes, and getting her hair done every week – and you know what a mess it used to look before.'

'I know who's told you that an' all,' Vicky said sharply. 'That Vera Bastowe from Admin. Wasn't it?'

'Yes, but how did you —?'

'How did I know? Because she went out with Tom Waldron twice, and then he never asked her again, and she's that peeved she does nothing but talk about him as if he was the last man on earth she'd ever fancy.'

They edged their way along the counter with their trays. Janet was bored by this talk – was there never anything to talk about but the other people in the firm? Oh, it was amusing sometimes, especially when Vicky was telling one of her absolutely incredible stories, and she knew that at times she, Janet, was guilty of the same thing. But after all, one couldn't gossip for ever without getting bored. At least, she couldn't.

'Bloody 'ell, shepherd's pie again,' Vicky remarked as they reached the meals section.

'You should have guessed – it was roast lamb yesterday. They've got to do something with the leftovers.'

'Well, I think I'll have the rissoles,' Vicky said.

'It makes no difference,' Janet said, 'it's all the same lamb.' She chose shepherd's pie and diced carrots, and plum pie and custard, and shuffled round to the cash desk to hand in her luncheon vouchers. As she sat down at a table with the other girls she stared at her tray with distaste. The battered metal tray, the thick white crockery, that Vicky had once said looked like misshapen chamber pots, the bent cutlery, and the dismal food – what would it be like to eat in some fabulous restaurant, with the pick of a huge menu? What a dream! She remembered Mrs. Landon saying how going away hadn't been the answer to her dreams. Well, maybe the high life didn't answer the cravings of your soul or whatever, but it must be nice just to try it, just once maybe.

Vicky and Nora had been chattering while she was daydreaming, and she was recalled by Vicky tapping her on the back of her hand with a fork.

up, Rip Van Winkle. Your dinner's getting cold.
ou dreamin' about anyway?'

actually,' Janet said, thrusting her fork into the
of her shepherd's pie.

Don't tell us you're going to the big city? Where
little girls get eaten alive. Where white slavers prowl the
streets looking for innocent young girls from Halifax and
Sheffield, and whip them off to South America? Where mad-
men with axes travel on the buses?' Vicky paused dramatic-
ally, fork clutched in one hand, waving her knife with the
other, and then unconcernedly carried on eating. 'Wouldn't
mind going there meself.'

'Well, I was thinking about it,' Janet said cautiously. 'Maybe just for a little while, to see what it's like. I'd like a change
from this place. Why, would you think of coming too?'

'Me? No!' Vicky said through a mouthful of rissoles and
chips. 'I know my place. I like being a big fish in a taddie-
pond. What was it that poet-fella said? Better to reign in hell
than snow in the south-east, sunny periods later, and you'll
need your umbrella for hailing taxis. I've heard of raining cats
and dogs, but hailing taxis is ridiculous.' She smiled round at
them. 'I do get carried away, don't I? But seriously, Jan, when
are you thinking of going?'

'I don't know yet,' Janet said. Above her the rain rattled on
the skylight, and two floors below, on her desk, a pile of invoices waited for her to check them. 'In a couple of weeks'
time I think.'

'So soon?' Vicky raised her eyebrows. 'Well, don't forget to
send us a postcard.'

'I haven't gone yet,' Janet said. She laughed uneasily. It
was almost as if Fate were pushing her into it, taking her a bit
too literally at her word. 'I don't know anyone down there to
go to.'

'Don't worry, something will. turn up,' Vicky said por-
tentously, and waved her knife over Janet's head. 'I can see
you are a young lass ripe for adventure, so as your fairy god-
mother I will give you a helping hand and with one wave of
my magic wand, change your head into a pumpkin – but wait,
I see Nature has got in before me!' She prodded up the last

14

few chips and transferred them to her mouth. 'Tell you what, though, Jan! You're probably wise to go down there for the winter. If it's anything like last winter, it's going to be like the Siberian Wastes up here.'

Four and a half months till Christmas. Rain and soot. Invoices. Rissoles and Irish stew. Phones ringing and internal memoranda. The Jack of Clubs Café and the all-night Horror Show at the Roxy. Fish fingers. Match of the day. Then it would snow and the buses would be diverted down St. Stephen's Avenue, and she'd have to walk the last half-mile home. Four and a half months till Christmas.

'I think I'll go,' Janet said.

CHAPTER TWO

Despite her resolution, Janet did nothing about it for some time. She didn't even mention it at home, for when she thought about it, she realized how much her mother and father liked having her there, now that her sister Sylvia had married and left. She was sure that they wouldn't stop her if she wanted to go, but until she had something definite in mind she thought it was just as well not to upset them. With these sort of considerations colouring her imagination, she even began to get cold feet, and to wonder if it was a sensible thing to consider, to leave home and go to London. By the end of the week she was in a state of complete uncertainty.

On the Sunday she and her parents were to go over to Sylvia's for lunch and to spend the afternoon. Sylvia and her husband, Geoff, lived in one of the houses on the new estate up the Adleigh Road, which for a start was enough to make Mum swell with pride, for she and Dad had lived all their lives in council houses, and thought of people who owned their own houses as being almost a race apart. Geoff was a senior draughtsman with Horton's, and doing pretty well, and Mum and Dad Anderson liked him well enough, though Dad had said on one occasion (and Janet had privately agreed with him) that there was a bit too much push and go-ahead about him for his liking.

It was raining again on Sunday when they set off, which annoyed Janet, for there was quite a walk from the bus stop to Sylvia's house, and she had just washed her hair the night before.

'It'll be a mess, one mass of frizz,' she complained to her mother as they stepped down from the bus.

'Can't you wash it again tonight, love?' her mother asked peaceably.

'No. That'd only make it worse. I can't wash it more than twice a week or there's no doing anything with it.'

16

'I can't see what you're worried about,' Dad said, glancing sideways at her. 'Allus looks all right to me. When I remember your mother, hours every night tryin' to get her hair to curl, and now here's you frettin' and cryin' because you can't keep it straight ... women!' Janet didn't bother to answer. She had heard all this before.

The estate was very new, and the houses and pavements looked clean and pinkish. The grass verges had taken at last, but the trees planted at regular intervals along the verge were still bare sticks propped up inside wire cages, and few of the gardens had anything growing in them.

'Be a time before they get anything to grow in them gardens,' Dad remarked as they walked down the road towards Sylvia's house. 'Nowt but stones. Terrible bit of soil. Couldn't grow slugs in it.'

'Geoffrey's done all right wi' his bit,' Mum said. She always felt she had to defend Geoff to her husband, even when he was not directly attacking him.

'Nasturtiums'll grow anywhere,' Dad replied briefly.

Geoff answered their ring at the door, and let them into the warm hallway that smelt of roasting meat.

'Syl's just putting the baby to bed,' he said as he ushered them in.

'Is she? Oh, I'd better go up and give her a hand,' Mum said eagerly. Dad raised his eyebrows at Geoff but neither of them pointed out that she had managed the task alone on countless occasions.

'Let's take your coat, Dad. Janet. How are you, Jan? Any exciting news?'

'Wish there was,' Janet said, shrugging her coat off and laying it over Geoff's arm. 'Nothing exciting ever happens to me.'

'Oh, there's plenty of time yet,' Geoff said pleasantly. 'Wait till you fall in love – everything'll seem exciting then. At least, so Sylvia tells me. Well, come on into the front room. We've got the fire lit today – it seemed so cold when we got up this morning.'

'It's as well to keep your fire goin' when it's as damp as this,' Dad agreed, and the two of them sat down for a male

17

natter. Janet wandered around the room looking at things. Sylvia and Geoff had done the house out nicely, and now Geoff had put up the shelving unit as a room divider between this and the dining area, there wasn't a thing needed doing in here. It must be nice, Janet thought, to have a room of your own to furnish and decorate as you wanted. Even though she had a bedroom of her own now, there was little that could be done with it; the furniture was old and heavy, and they couldn't afford to throw it away and buy new stuff; and because it was so big, and the room so small, there was only one possible arrangement of the pieces so that they would all fit in. The only thing that Janet could do about her room was choose the colour of the distemper, and that wasn't much.

A few minutes later Mum and Sylvia came downstairs, having settled the baby for the afternoon. Sylvia was four years older than Janet, a tall, pretty, dark-haired girl, who had always been much admired, popular at school and with the boys and obviously a candidate for early marriage. In fact she had only had to work for eighteen months before getting engaged, and when Geoff had married her she had left work for good to be a housewife.

'Hello Jan – hello Dad. Haven't you got the drinks out yet, Geoff? Shame on you. I'd like a sherry, if no-one else would!' Sylvia said.

'Sorry, love, I forgot – so interested in what Dad was saying. Anyone else like a drink? Mum, how about a sherry for you?'

'Not for me, thanks love. It'd make me fall asleep.'

'I wouldn't mind a glass o' beer if you've got one, Geoffrey,' Dad said.

'Sherry for you, Jan?'

'Mm, please.'

'Don't you ever feel strange, doing things like this?' Janet asked Sylvia when they were all seated again with their drinks. 'I mean, imagine having sherry before lunch in Burton Street – it just wouldn't go, would it?'

'There were lots of things we did at home that I wouldn't do now,' Sylvia said, 'and vice versa, but I don't feel strange, no. It's different living here, different area, different sort of house.

18

If I was at home in Burton Street now I'd quite happily hang my washing over the horse in front of the kitchen fire – here I'd never do that in a million years.'

'You'll find out when you've a home of your own, Janet,' Mum said. 'I was the very same way. When I left my mother to set up home with your father, I did things all my own way, and thought what my mother had been doing for fifty years wasn't good enough for me.'

'I can't see me ever having a home of my own,' Janet said gloomily. 'The way things are going I shall end up an old maid with a fat cat.'

Sylvia laughed. 'You're young yet.'

'You can talk! You were two years married by the time you'd got to my age.'

'Yes, but what goes for one doesn't go for another. You've had time to enjoy life as a single girl, look around a bit and so on —'

'Look around a bit! All I've ever seen is this town, and you could look around that in an hour and a half on a Saturday morning. You don't need four years for *that*.'

'You have got the blues good and proper,' Sylvia said. 'It sounds to me as if she's working up to something, eh, Mum?'

'She's had her cold this summer. It's the wet weather 'at's getting her down, I suppose,' Mum said. Janet looked at them, both staring at her like a pair of dairymen looking at a sick cow, and she began to laugh.

'That's better,' Sylvia said. 'How about coming into the kitchen and talking to me while I do the sprouts? Doing good turns is supposed to make you feel good.'

The kitchen was warm and smelt of food and the windows were pleasantly steamed-up, so that once they had the door shut they felt cosy and private for a heart to heart chat. Sylvia got the sprouts into a bowl and started to trim them with a sharp knife, and then said,

'All right, out with it.'

'Out with what?' Janet asked innocently.

'What's all the gloom and despondency for? Boy trouble?'

'I haven't got one – at least, not a special one.'

'Well, what is it then? You nearly had Mum taking your

19

temperature in there.'

'Oh, I'm just fed up, Syl. Nothing ever seems to happen to me. I just go to work, come home and watch the telly, and then go to bed. Day after day.'

'And what are you going to do about it?'

'Well, I had thought of going away for a bit, but —'

'But what?' Sylvia prompted kindly.

'Well, I wondered how Mum and Dad would take it. And then I started to get cold feet, wondering how I'd make out on my own, and wondering if I wouldn't just end up doing exactly the same things in some other town.'

'Where were you thinking of going?'

'Well, London, I suppose, but —'

'No sense in doing things by half. If you're going to go away, you might as well go to the biggest. I think it's a good idea.'

'Do you really?' Janet asked, grateful and surprised.

'Yes, really. You obviously need a change, to stretch your wings and so on. Get a bit of excitement before you settle down. I don't regret for a minute getting married and starting a family, but sometimes I'd give my eye teeth for the freedom you've got.'

'But I've done nothing with it.'

'There's still time. Where were you planning to stay?'

'Well, I hadn't got as far as making any plans. I don't think I know anyone in London, and I don't fancy going down there on the off-chance of finding a flat vacant.'

'I think you're right there. Well, I can't help you at the moment, but I'll ask around, and get Geoff to do the same. We might be able to come up with something.'

'Thanks, Syl.'

'And don't worry too much about Mum and Dad. I think they must realize by now that you won't stay for ever. As long as you don't do anything silly, I don't think they'll worry.'

'You're a good friend, Sylvia.'

'That's what sisters are for. How about laying the table for me in return while I finish off the veggies?'

The chat with Sylvia did a lot to settle Janet's mind, but still she didn't mention the matter to her parents, and the problem of where she could live in London seemed no nearer to being settled. However, it was only the following Friday that something happened. Janet had just arrived at work, and was in the cloakroom combing her hair when Vicky dashed in, early to work for probably the first time in a month.

'Ey-up, there you are then?'

'What are you doing here?' Janet asked with assumed astonishment. 'It's only five to nine. You should still be in bed.'

'I know, I caught the wrong bus by mistake. No, shut up a minute. Remember you were talking about going to London?'

'Yes.'

'Were you serious?'

'Yes.'

'Have you done anything about it?'

'No.'

'Then I've got something here that might interest you.'

'What is it?'

'Hang on a jiff while I take me coat off – right, now come with me to my office where it's a bit private – no-one from Despatch ever comes in till a quarter past.'

Janet followed her along the corridor and into the long musty Despatch office, with its bare lino floor and old wooden desks, much hacked about with penknives, looking so much like a council school. Vicky sat down on the edge of her own desk and rummaged in her handbag and finally produced a letter.

'Now,' she said, 'do you remember Sandra Barclay?'

'Who?'

'Sandra Barclay – at school, you twit.'

'Oh yes, of course. She was in your class.'

'That's right. Well, she lives in London – she's been there for nearly two years now – and she writes to me now and again.'

'I didn't think you were that friendly with her,' Janet said.

'We weren't really bosom buddies at school, but we both left at the same time and went to the secretarial course, so we got friendly. She's quite a nice sort really. Anyway, when I got home last night there was this letter waiting for me.'

21

'From Sandra.'

'From Sandra. How perceptive you are, Holmes. And guess what?'

'She's asked you to marry her.'

'Not a bad guess,' Vicky said solemnly, 'but wrong. Guess again.'

'Oh *tell* me, for heaven's sake,' Janet said, exasperated.

'All right. Sandra shares this flat with another girl, and apparently this other girl is leaving in a fortnight's time. She says it's a nuisance because it means advertising, and getting a stranger to share, which she doesn't like the idea of, and she's a bit worried in case she can't get anyone straight away, because she can't afford the rent on her own.'

'So you thought —'

'So I thought maybe if I wrote to her and suggested you shared with her, she might welcome you with open arms.'

'If she hasn't already got someone.'

'And if you can go down there in two weeks' time.'

'And if I can afford the rent. I suppose she doesn't mention how much it is?'

'No. What about it then?'

'I'd really like to think about it,' Janet said doubtfully. She didn't like the feeling of being rushed into making the decision.

'Ah, come on, where's your spirit of adventure? Do things on the spur of the moment, like I do. They always turn out better. Or nearly always,' honesty compelled her to add. 'Anyway, there isn't time to be cautious. If you want to try it, I'll have to write to her today so she'll get it tomorrow, because I expect she'll put an advertisement in on Monday.'

'Well, I don't know,' Janet dithered.

'What's the problem? Could you be ready to leave in two weeks? You only have to give a week's notice here, and you won't want to do much packing, and you haven't even got a steady boy-friend.'

'Oh, I suppose I could without too much trouble.'

'Well then, what else is there to worry about?'

'I'll need a job,' Janet began, but Vicky broke in with, 'Don't worry about that. Anyone can get a job down there.

All you've got to do is walk into an agency as soon as you arrive, and they'll have a job lined up for you for the next day. You might have to work a week's lying time, but then you'll have your week's lying-time from here, and your holiday pay—'

'I've had my holiday.'

'Yes, but you've your third week to come. They'll pay you that.'

'I've got some savings anyway. Enough to get by on.'

'Well, there you are then. What's to worry about?'

'It's just that – well, it's so sudden.'

'Well, why not? It isn't a life-or-death decision. Come on girl, it's a great chance. You might not get another – I mean, how many people do you know who live in London?'

'None. All right, Vicky. You write to her, and if she says yes, and I can afford the rent, I'll do it.'

'Good girl!' Vicky jumped up, clapped her on the back and did a little dance for joy.

'You seem very eager to get rid of me,' Janet said suspiciously.

'Oh, I am, I am. I want to snatch Spotty away from you while you're in the Wicked City. Besides, with you living down there I'm all set up for weekend trips, no hotel bills. You wouldn't refuse your Aunt Vicky a kip on the floor, would you? And a crust off your table?' she crooned. Janet laughed.

'Hold on, I haven't got there yet – but if it does work out, I hope you will come and stay for a weekend – I should miss you if you didn't.'

'Well,' Vicky said with satisfaction, 'and that's more than Sandra ever said, the bitch, and she's been there for two years. You can easily tell who your real friends are. Ey-up, here come the others. It must be late.'

'Oh god, it's a quarter past nine,' Janet exclaimed in horror. 'Are you coming in to me for coffee or will I come to you?' she asked over her shoulder as she dashed for the door.

'I'll come in to you,' Vicky said, unconcernedly lighting a cigarette. 'You've got carpet in your office.' She looked up and caught the astonished gaze of her immediate superior. 'Morning, Mr. Cross. And the first person to make a crack

23

about me being early, I'll stub my fag out on his hand.'

Vicky wrote the letter, put it through the firm's franking machine, and posted it at lunchtime, and the reply came back promptly, and was waiting for her when she got home on Monday night. She brought the letter to work with her on Tuesday and showed it to Janet at the coffee break.

'There you are, it sounds perfect,' Vicky said, and then, noticing the open door behind Janet's desk, turned her back on it and continued in a lower voice. 'She says it's five pounds a week, plus a share of the gas and electricity bills, and she says that would come to about ten bob a week. And you'd have your own room, and share kitchen, bathroom and sitting room. Perfect. Here's the bit I like, though – "I remember Janet Anderson as being very quiet and tidy. Tell her if she likes it it's hers, but I must know by return either way." Very quiet and tidy! That's a deliberate stab at me, you know. What she really wants to say is that it's a good job I wasn't applying for myself because she wouldn't have me if I was gold-plated.'

'Five pounds. That doesn't sound like much. I was expecting it to be much more. I should be able to manage easily.'

'Well, I'll write and tell her it's on, then?'

'Oh, I'll have to speak to my parents first,' Janet said.

'They wouldn't stop you, would they?' Vicky asked, surprised.

'Oh no – I'm sure they'll agree, only it would upset them if they thought I'd made all the arrangements without consulting them.'

'Well, they don't have to think that, do they? I'll write off to Sandra, and you can take this letter home and show them and ask them – you don't have to tell them you've already written.'

'I didn't think of that,' Janet said.

'Course you didn't. And why?'

'Because I'm honest.'

'Because you're daft,' Vicky corrected. 'Eh, you'll make sure and write to us, won't you?'

'Steady on. I haven't gone yet.'

It took Janet a whole evening to get her parents used to the idea. They, like her, thought at first that the whole thing was too sudden, but when she reasonably pointed out that it would make no difference if she was to go in a week's time or a year's time, they had to concede her point.

'And Sandra's been there for two years, so she'll be able to show me around. It's not as though I'll be alone.'

'What about a job? Have you thought o' that?' Dad asked, sucking meditatively on his pipe.

'There's plenty of jobs for girls down there, especially typists and so on. Vicky says you can just walk into an agency and start a job right away.'

'And what does Vicky know about it?' Mum asked sharply. She didn't much approve of Vicky Duke's ways.

'What Sandra's told her,' Janet said quickly. 'They're crying out for typists and secretaries in London. Anyway, even if I have to wait a week before I start a job, I'll still manage. I'll have my week's lying-time, and holiday pay, and my savings. There's nothing to worry about, really.'

Dad was silent for a moment, and then said slowly, 'I think it'll be all right, mother. She's a sensible lass, she's never given us any cause for worry. After all, they've all got to try their wings some time.'

'I suppose so,' Mum said doubtfully. 'Well, as long as you ring us up now and then – Mrs. Anson won't mind us poppin' in there for a call – and write to us every week —'

'Of course I'll write to you,' Janet said.

'And you can come home whenever you like – your room'll be ready, you know.'

'All right, mother, she hasn't gone yet, and you're talking about her coming back,' Dad interrupted.

'Well, she has to know this is her home.'

'I know, Mum, and thanks. Don't worry about me, I'll be very sensible.'

There was one more interview before the thing was finally settled, and that took place the following day. Janet wrote her letter of resignation first thing the next morning and sealed it in an envelope, and as soon as there was a quiet moment she took it in to Mrs. Landon.

'Yes, Janet, what can I do for you?' she asked pleasantly.

'I was wondering if you could tell me who I should give this to?'

25

'What is it?'

'My letter of resignation,' Janet said. Mrs. Landon looked surprised for a moment, and then smiled.

'So you're going after all! To London?'

'Yes. A friend of Vicky's down there is going to share a flat with me.'

'When are you leaving?'

'Friday week.'

Mrs. Landon nodded. 'Got a job yet?'

'No, but it's easy enough to get a job down there.'

'Yes, I suppose it is. Well, I'm very pleased for you, and I hope you have a wonderful time.'

'Thank you. Er – this letter. . . ?'

'Oh yes, of course, I'm sorry. Well, it should go to Mr. Tomlinson, and a copy to Personnel – did you do it in duplicate?'

'No, I didn't know.'

'Well, go through next door and make a photocopy of it, and then you can take the copy straight up to Mrs. Burrows, and I'll drop the original in to Mr. Tomlinson – that way you won't have to talk to him about it.'

'Thanks,' Janet smiled. 'I was rather dreading that.'

'He does tend to get carried away at times,' Mrs. Landon smiled sympathetically. 'By the way – you remember what I said to you before on the subject of going to London?'

'Yes – about keeping enough back to come home if I didn't like it.'

'Mm. Well, I'm sure you won't want to, but if you do want to come back and you need a job, just give me a ring. I can always get you in somewhere at Emerson's.'

'Thanks – thanks a lot. I'll remember,' Janet said. Everything was being made very easy for her – even her escape route was being mapped out, in case the adventure should go wrong. This wasn't Vicky's idea of the thing at all. She should be heading off into the unknown with nothing but the clothes she stood up in, and no chance of ever returning, to satisfy Vicky's notion of adventure. However, Janet was the one who was going, and on the whole she thought she preferred it this way.

CHAPTER THREE

It wasn't a particularly auspicious start. To begin with, Janet had a hangover from her farewell party on Friday night, organized by Vicky. She hadn't much wanted to go, but she could hardly refuse without being all sorts of a meanie, and Vicky had so plainly been looking forward to it. All the girls she knew, and a lot of the boys, especially from the packaging shop, in whose canteen she and Vicky sometimes played darts in the lunch-hour, turned out, and Janet was quite touched, not having realized how popular she was. The result of it was that she got a little carried away and drank far more than she meant to, and now she had a raging head, a thirst like the Kalahari, and a feeling of general depression and gloom, mixed with the excitement which she had expected to feel. This was how a bridegroom must feel on his way to the wedding, she thought, with his hangover from the stag-party.

Fortunately she had done her packing on Thursday night, all except small essentials like toothbrush and sponge-bag. Sylvia and Geoff had given her a pretty little leather overnight bag as a goodbye present, which had compartments for brush and comb, make-up, soap and so on, and was ready supplied with a spare pair of one-size tights, and a packet of throw-away knickers (which Janet thought privately were rather horrible, but she admitted reluctantly they might conceivably be useful some time) and into this she had shoved the things which were not packed in her two suitcases. Janet had been very strict with herself over the packing, and had made two lists before the final one that she used. Mum had said several times that it didn't matter much if she forgot anything because she could always come up and collect it at the weekends; and Janet had seen this as a plot by her mother to keep the ties with home and make London only a week-day stopping place, so she had firmly vowed to herself that whatever she forgot she would do without.

Of course, it couldn't really be like going away for good, because there was so much that she had to leave behind for Mum and Dad to look after – her old dolls and schoolbooks, her records and novels, lots of clothes that she rarely wore but didn't want to throw away, her box of letters, all sorts of odds and ends, the old treasures that made up her past. Where these things were was her home, however much she might tell herself differently, and until she had a place of her own with room to keep all these bits and pieces, Burton Street would remain her home and wherever she lived would only be a temporary stopping-place. Probably Mum realized this as well, for she was remarkably calm on Saturday morning when she and Dad waved goodbye on the central station platform.

Mum and Dad's present to her was a new coat, which she was wearing, since the day was cool, and it cheered her up a little, but only at first. There was nobody even remotely interesting in her carriage, so from that point of view the new coat was wasted. The carriage was warm and stuffy, and seemed to grow more so as they moved south, the greyness of the day made the scenery uninteresting, and her hangover grew progressively worse. There were delays all along the line, which made the journey even longer and more tedious than it need have been, so by the time the train pulled into Euston, Janet was very much in need of cheering up. Sandra was supposed to be meeting her from the train, but as it was by now three-quarters of an hour late, Janet felt that she would probably not have waited, and was wondering if she would be able to find her way to the flat on her own, or would she have to take a taxi, and how much would it cost?

Janet had – typical luck! – got in at the back of the train, and so had to walk the whole length of the platform with her cases, so by the time she got to the ticket barrier most of the crowd had dispersed. She handed in her ticket, walked through, and dumped her cases down and looked around. There were several people hanging about, but none of them looked at her, and none of them looked remotely familiar. I suppose, she thought doubtfully, we will recognize each other when we see each other. She may be late too – I'd better wait a while. She shuffled her cases out of the way and stood in front

28

of them, as prominently as she dared. The huge new station was thronging with people, and she was amazed at how many Irish accents she heard around her. Even the train-announcer was an Irish girl. She supposed the trains must go from here to Ireland. There was a buffet over there – she was gasping for a cup, but she dared not leave her place in case Sandra came and missed her. It was much warmer here than it had been at home – she supposed it must be because they were further south. But she was really in London at last! A belated wave of excitement swept over her, momentarily overcoming the depression and tiredness.

She had been waiting for about fifteen minutes, and was beginning to worry again about how to get to the flat on her own, when she saw a girl coming across the open space towards her, a smart, dark-haired girl in long boots and a camel-coloured coat, who was looking at her with an expression of friendly enquiry. Janet smiled uncertainly.

'Hello – it is Janet Anderson, isn't it?'

'Yes – you're Sandra,' Janet said, though it was really more of a question than a statement. She didn't recognize this girl at all.

'Sorry you've had to wait. Your train was so late I had to go and get a cup of coffee – I simply couldn't stand there a minute longer. You must have come in while I was in the buffet.'

'I was afraid you'd got fed up and gone home, the train was so late,' Janet said. Now she had had a good look at her, she could just trace a resemblance to the Sandra Barclay she remembered, but it was far from obvious, even allowing for the different hairstyle and the smart make-up – far more of it than even Vicky wore. As if she had read her thoughts, Sandra said, 'I don't expect you recognized me – the last time I saw you I still had my hair in plaits. I'd have known you anywhere though – you haven't changed a bit.'

Now was there a slight hint of pity in that remark? Janet thought, and then stopped herself. Really, Janet Anderson, don't be so stupidly touchy. It's just because you've got a hangover.

'You have changed,' Janet admitted, 'but then I didn't know

29

you awfully well at school so I probably don't remember properly.'

'No, you used to go around with Jacky Hill's crowd, didn't you? Here, I'll take one of those —' She picked up one of the suitcases. 'We have to get the tube – this way.'

Sandra led the way out of the station, walking briskly, and Janet fell in beside her. Outside the day was grey and hot, that muggy sort of heat that made you feel tired and dirty. The traffic roared past on the big main road, and the buildings were tall and very dirty; it was so noisy that neither of them spoke at first. Janet said at last, 'Is it far?'

'Is what far?' Sandra asked.

'The flat.'

'Oh, not really. Round that corner there, we get the tube and then it's straight through to Ladbroke Grove. Then it's about five minutes from the station at the other end.'

'Oh,' Janet said, still having no idea how far it was. It took her some time before she got used to the lack of measure of distance in London. Travelling by tube, one lost the sense of how far one place was from another, and distance tended to be measured in time – 'it's only half an hour on the tube' and so on. But for a long time she found it odd and confusing.

The underground was quite interesting to her, and though she didn't like the smell and the heat and the jostle, she found the automatic doors fascinating. They didn't talk much in the train, and Janet noticed that none of the other passengers spoke either, which was quite different from the buses at home, where everyone yelled over the top of everyone else. She read the advertisements. Two headless girls had a very phoney chat about something called Brook Street Bureau. A sprightly girl in headphones smiled from beneath the caption 'Good morning, operator'. Another well-made-up girl decided she wanted to be a bank manager, and explained in half-sentences that it was quite possible at *her* bank. Yet another was framed against a blue sky and gazed into the distance at her rosy future from beneath the peak of a traffic-warden's cap. Vicky was right, there were plenty of jobs. 'Moira Fitzgibbon likes Nina Simone.' Who cares? Certainly not Nina Simone, nor I. 'Château Lafitte'. Château La Feet. Like the dreadful meal

Mum used to threaten us with as kids when we wouldn't eat what we were given – toenail soup and old man's leg. She turned to Sandra, who was staring ahead of her with a glazed expression of patience, like most of the other people in the carriage.

'There seem to be a lot of adverts about jobs for women – is it easy to get a job?'

'Mm? – oh yes, there are plenty of office jobs about. There always seems to be a labour shortage in London, though it's not as easy for the men I don't think. You can type, can't you?'

'Yes, but I'm really a machinist. You know – Burroughs and so on.'

'Oh well, you'll have no trouble getting something. Really it's only the girls who can't do anything that have to worry – but even then, they can always get a job in a shop – you know, check-out operator and that sort of thing.'

'Is it best to go to an agency?' Janet wanted to know. She didn't like the adverts, they irritated her, but if it was safer that way she was willing to patronize them.

'If you like. Some people look in the papers, but I don't think it matters much, except that it's probably less trouble to go to an agency. They do all the phoning up for you, that sort of thing.'

'What do you do?' Janet wanted to know.

'I work for the B.B.C.,' Sandra said, with a hint of importance in her voice.

'As a secretary?'

'Assistant, it's called, but it's much the same thing.'

'Did you go through an agency?'

'No, I heard about it from a friend, but I have used an agency before. If you don't know what you want to do, I should try temping for a while. The pay's better, and it isn't so boring, moving around all the time.'

'That's an idea,' Janet said thoughtfully. 'I don't really know what I want to do – I'd really like a complete change, though what to I don't know.'

'I expect something'll turn up,' Sandra said vaguely, turning her head away. She had looked in that direction several times while they were talking, and Janet at last realized what

31

she was doing – she was looking at her own reflection in the glass partition at the end of the row of seats. Janet gave a small smile to herself. She was beginning to get an inkling of what Sandra Barclay was like now she had 'grown up'.

During the last part of the journey the train came up above ground, and the stations they passed through seemed to get older and dirtier, and the people who got on to the train at these stations seemed poorer and worse-dressed. At last Sandra nudged her and said 'This is ours', and as she stood up and led the way to the door the train slowed and drew into Ladbroke Grove station. This is it, thought Janet. They made their way down the echoing wooden steps and out on to the street, and again Janet found herself almost stunned by the noise. Cars rushed past in both directions, the pavements were solid with people, and the grey muggy heat hung over everything in a depressing sort of way.

'Is it always like this?' she asked Sandra as she hopped about in her wake, and Sandra, dodging through the pedestrians with practised ease, shouted over her shoulder, 'Like what?'

'So crowded?'

'I suppose so. It's a bit worse today, p'raps, because of the market, and everyone's out shopping. It's quiet on Sundays though.'

The crowd thinned out as they walked away from the station, and Janet was able to fall in beside her companion and look around her. There were tall plane trees on either side of the road, with massive, peeling trunks and yellow-green leaves hanging limp, but they were the only thing of beauty to see. The houses must once have been impressive, but were now drab, neglected, some nearly derelict. Old rusty cars were parked at both sides of the roads, along with some new and flashy models. The pavements were covered in litter and dog-dirt. She had thought her own home-town was dirty and drab, but this was far worse. Sandra turned off the main road into a side road much the same, except that the houses seemed even more derelict – several of them, indeed, had their doors and windows boarded up with corrugated iron, and there were 'For Sale' notices up in front of others. Broken-down walls partly

32

protected ragged privet-hedges that smelt strongly of cats. Sandra led the way past a group of very dirty children playing hopscotch on the pavement, and one of them looked up and said ' 'lo Sarnge,' as they passed.

'This is it,' Sandra said, stopping in front of a gateway. 'Ours is on the top floor.'

Janet looked up at the house. The plaster was peeling off the front in great patches. The window frames needed painting, the stone walls in front and flanking the steps up to the front door needed repairing. The front door stood open, like most of the doors on the street, and inside it was very dark and rather evil-smelling, and there were no fewer than three semi-dismembered prams blocking the hallway. Sandra climbed over them without a word and began to climb the stairs, and Janet followed, feeling close to tears and wondering why she had ever come.

Inside, the flat was not marvellous, but it was so much better than the outside of the house had led her to expect that Janet felt it was near perfect.

'This will be your room,' Sandra said, opening a door to the left of the front door. 'It's a bit bare – I didn't know Betty owned so much of the furniture until she started clearing it out. Still, you can pick up bits of furniture quite cheap in the market.'

Bare it certainly was. It was a long narrow slip of a room, windowless, but with a glass fanlight above the door, which probably meant it had been the nursery once, and it contained nothing but a divan bed, a rickety wooden chair and an old-fashioned wardrobe. However, the walls seemed to have been recently distempered, and there was a fawn-coloured carpet on the floor which was still in very good condition.

'I like it,' Janet said. Sandra raised one eyebrow in faint surprise at this reaction, but she could not know that Janet was already seeing it as it would look when she had finished, with the chair and wardrobe painted white, a new white chest of drawers, a floor-length, brightly coloured bedspread, pictures on the walls ... 'In a way, I'm glad there isn't much furniture – it will give me the chance to furnish it how I like. I never could at home, all the furniture was already there.'

'Mm, I suppose so,' the other girl said, unconvinced. 'I can lend you a pair of sheets for the moment, but I'll need them back by Thursday, so I can wash them for the weekend.'

'Thanks. I can buy a pair through the week.'

'Well, dump your case and come and see the rest of the flat – what there is of it.' Sandra led the way back out into the passage, which formed a T shape, with the front door at its foot. Turning to the left and then straight ahead they went into Sandra's bedroom. It was much bigger than Janet's, square, and with a large window that looked out into the tangled back gardens of the houses on this side and backing on opposite. The room was cluttered, and there were discarded clothes everywhere, on the bed, on the floor, over chairs, even on the window-sill.

'It's a bit of a mess at the moment,' Sandra apologized off-handedly. 'You see, I change every evening when I come in from work, and I never seem to have time to put one set of clothes away as I put another lot on.'

'So I see,' Janet said, grinning. She was remembering Sandra's comment in her letter to Vicky about tidiness, and as if Sandra read her mind, she went on, 'Betty and I made it a rule that we tidied up as we went along in the shared part of the flat, even if we made a mess in our own rooms, and it always worked well.'

'That's fine by me,' Janet said. 'I prefer things tidy.'

'Well, come and see the sitting room.' This was the room opposite the front door. Again it was square, with one large window commanding the same view, and was furnished with three large sagging chairs and an ancient sofa, all covered with home-made chintz loose-covers, presumably to disguise the state they were in underneath. The carpet was dark blue, and matched the full-length curtains. There was a book-case with the glass missing, filled with paperbacks, and a coffee table covered in old magazines, and in the corner standing on an orange-box there was a television, topped by the usual tangle of aerials.

'Very nice,' Janet said vaguely. She couldn't somehow see herself in here, feeling at home, but perhaps that would come.

The kitchen was opposite Sandra's bedroom, at the other

34

end of the T. The lino-tiles on the floor had had a bashing, and two of them were missing altogether. The walls were peeling and looked damp, and the plaster round the sink had come off in great evil-looking chunks. There was a gas-stove and a fridge, and a wooden table and three wooden chairs, and a 'unit' – work-surface above, two drawers and two cupboards below.

'This will be your cupboard, for keeping food in, I mean. The saucepans and so on are under the sink, cutlery in this drawer.'

'We each cook our own then?' Janet asked. She had been wondering how this would be arranged, for never having shared a flat she couldn't imagine anyone cooking for themselves and not for the other person in the house. It would seem mean, somehow.

'Well, Betty and I took turns doing breakfast, and we each used to cook our own tea because she came in from work earlier than me. At weekends it was just whoever happened to feel like it. We didn't have a set arrangement.'

'I see,' Janet said, feeling that that wasn't very helpful.

'Now you've seen everything – oh, except the bathroom. That's next door – here. Very ordinary you see,' and she flung open the door, giving Janet a glimpse of blue-painted walls, an old-fashioned claw-footed bath, geyser on the wall, toilet, washstand. Very ordinary indeed.

'So there we are,' Sandra shut the door again and looked at Janet as if expecting a verdict. Janet smiled uncertainly.

'Yes, thank you,' was all she could think of to say.

'You'll soon settle in. Oh, remind me to give you the keys. There's a key to the door downstairs, though it's nearly always left open, but you might sometimes find it shut if you come in late at night. We had to put a new lock on our door up here; Betty lost so many keys I should think half of London could have got in. You don't lose keys, do you?'

'Not that I know of,' Janet said, thinking, if she doesn't suggest a cup of tea soon I shall go home. Oh, come on, no sense in being shy with the girl. You live here now. Out with it, girl. 'How about a cup of tea?'

'Oh, of course. Well, coffee actually. Don't have tea. Betty never drank it, and I can't be bothered with all that mucking about and getting rid of tea leaves and so on. But there is a teapot somewhere if you want to make it for yourself some time.'

Over a cup of instant coffee (which was so very instant that Janet resolved to make a quarter of tea her first purchase) Sandra chatted about various matters like the delivery of milk, and quarterly gas and electricity bills, where the nearest telephone kiosk and shops were, and so on. She seemed to like her position as mentor and information desk, and Janet, knowing nothing about London, was willing enough to provide her with questions and an audience. But Sandra was very much a stranger to her. It was impossible to read anything of her character, and Janet had not known her well enough at school to be able to guess at it. I suppose, she thought, I'll get to know her better. I hope so, at least, because she's the only person in the whole of London that I know. And just for a moment, she caught herself wishing that Vicky was there.

CHAPTER FOUR

'God, it's nearly half past four,' Sandra exclaimed. 'I'd better show you the shops if you want to get some food in before they shut.'

'That's a point,' Janet said. 'I suppose you've done your shopping?'

'Yes, I did it this morning. I don't mind going round with you, though. Shall I lend you a shopping bag?'

Sandra led the way back towards the station, pointing things out en route with a kind of proprietary pride that amused Janet, though she did not let it show.

'That's the new motorway – the number seven bus-stop – David Greig's, I do most of my shopping in there – quite a good baker's – Notting Hill Gate's up that way ... some fairly decent pubs up there – we'll just take a quick look at the market.'

'Market?' Janet asked dutifully.

'Portobello Market. It's one of the most famous street-markets in London. Fruit and vegetables, and antiques. You could probably get some bits and pieces for your room there. There aren't many real bargains there now – too many people have got to know about it – but there's still some good stuff, if you've got the eye for it.'

Janet listened as she trotted obediently in Sandra's wake. She had bought the things she thought she needed to see her over the weekend, and had been stunned by the prices. She had never really thought much about the price of food, though of course she had heard her mother complaining about it daily for as long as she could remember. It was an eye-opener. She was going to have to be careful in future. The market she loved. It was just like the street market at home, only much bigger and noisier, and of course with the addition of antique shops. The accents of the stall-holders fascinated her – she could hardly understand a word they said. Sandra, she noticed, had lost almost all her native accent, and Janet wondered if she would lose hers. She thought she would not mind, if she ended up speaking like these wizened wizards who flung fruit and vegetables about like jugglers and kept up a stream of unintelligible chatter like a cage full of mynas.

They walked part of the way down, and then Sandra turned back, saying, 'I'll have to get back. I must have something to eat and have a bath before I go out.' A thought seemed to strike her. 'I don't suppose you've got anything to do this evening, have you?'

'Well, no, apart from unpacking.'

'Would you like to come with me? I'm going to the club for a drink with a few friends – you can come along if you like.'

'That's very nice of you. What club's that?'

'Oh, the B.B.C. club, at the Television Centre, where I work. It's quite a nice place, and they have a terrace looking over the park where we usually sit when it's warm. I can introduce you to a few people.'

'Thanks very much,' Janet said, feeling cheered. The idea of a drink on a terrace looking over a park was much nicer than the idea of unpacking in her bare little room and then watching television. She wished she could get rid of the uncharitable feeling that Sandra was doing all these things just to impress her. It was a very unworthy thought, but there was something about the way she spoke, about the flourish in her voice, and the way she emphasized certain words that made Janet feel she was enjoying the role, and wasn't really interested in how she, Janet, felt.

Back at the flat Sandra turned the bath on and ate baked beans on toast while it was filling. Janet started her unpacking, and then while Sandra was in the bath, she cooked herself egg on toast and bacon and sausage, and had a whole delicious pot of tea, and after that felt very cheerful. Sandra was ages in the bath, and finally emerged in clouds of steam like a pantomime devil and padded wetly to her bedroom, shutting the door after her. A moment later her head came round the door and she yelled, 'Janet, can you hand me in my brush? I left it on the bathroom shelf.' The bare arm was hanging round the door, hand open to receive, when Janet approached with the brush, and asked as she handed it over, 'By the way, how smart is this club? What sort of thing should I wear?'

The arm retreated and the head reappeared. Sandra's face looked strangely small without all that make-up, and, to Janet, almost embarrassingly human.

'Well, it is pretty smart,' she said ruminatively. 'I mean, not sequins or cocktail dress or that sort o' style, but not jeans or skirt-and-jumper either.'

'I think I get the idea,' Janet said, noticing with amusement how the trace of the northern accent came back when the face-mask was off. Very odd!

The two girls set off at twenty past seven in the warm muggy evening, to catch a number seven bus to the end of North Pole Road, where Sandra spotted a 220 coming and dragged Janet off.

'Saves us a walk,' she said, running across the road to the other bus stop as well as she could in her very high heels.

Janet was most impressed with the round television building, and despite herself was impressed with Sandra's air as she took Janet past the commissionaire, and led the way through corridors and up in the lift to the top floor. Sandra got her past the large bearded man who guarded the entrance to the bar, and led the way in with what was very nearly a swagger.

'There they are, over there,' she murmured, and propelled Janet quickly across to a group sitting round a table by the open french windows, three very smart men and two very smart girls, who waved to Sandra as she approached and greeted her loudly.

'About time, Sandy, we were giving you up. What'll you have to drink, love?' This from a tall, fair-haired young man who stood up and gave Sandra a flourishing kiss on the cheek as he spoke.

'I see you've brought us some new blood,' said another, a small boy who looked as if he was Chinese, but spoke with a London accent. 'Do introduce us.'

'Oh yes, this is Janet who went to the same school as me. She's just come down to share my flat. Jan, this is Andy,' the

Chinese boy, 'and Pete,' the fair-haired one, 'and Dave, Sally and Sue.'

They nodded to each other, and Dave murmured, 'How d'you do', but Andy said in a loud voice, 'Super, love. Come and sit down by me, Janet, and tell me all about yourself. Pete, get her a drink, don't just stand about there looking lovely. Ignore these people,' to Janet again, 'they aren't worth bothering about. I'm the only one here worth talking to.'

'Don't mind the yellow peril,' Pete said, 'he fancies himself as a wolf. What would you like to drink, dear?'

Janet didn't know, of course, what sort of thing people drank here, so after a hesitation she said, 'A half of lager, please,' thinking that it was a nice safe choice.

'How delightfully quaint, a lady draught-drinker,' Andy said loudly. 'Sandy dear, I think I'm going to like your flatmate.'

'They don't have draught lager here,' Pete interrupted, trying to be kind. 'Will a bottle do?'

'Yes, thank you.'

'Usual for me, Pete,' Sandra said and sat down next to the girls, so that the only seat left was the one Pete had vacated, next to Andy. Blast, Janet thought, I'm going to get stuck with this would-be funny guy.

'Snuggle up then, love, and tell me all about yourself,' Andy said, and as she sat, unwillingly, in the chair beside him, he hitched his own a little nearer to hers.

'There's nothing to tell,' Janet said sharply, and then, knowing that this would not discourage him for an instant, she tried to distract his attention by a question. 'What do you do here? Are you an actor?'

'Me? Of course not. Do I look like one?' He sounded genuinely surprised.

'I don't know what you mean – what does an actor look like?'

'Sweetie, they're all as queer as nine-bob notes, surely you knew that?'

Janet burst out laughing, and said, 'What nonsense!' so firmly that Andy was taken aback for a moment, and then said to her in a low voice, meant only for her ears, 'D'you know, you're the first person who's said nonsense to me since I left the Boy Scouts. I think I'm going to like you, Miss Leeds 1973.'

Ah, now I know how to handle him – he's one of these people who likes to be insulted – thinks it's amusing. All right, laddie, here goes —

'But I'm quite sure I'm not going to like you,' she said, with far more sincerity than he would ever credit her for: his reaction was to laugh loudly, and pat her hand.

'Lovely, lovely. But now, here comes your drink in its frosted flagon. Drink it nicely and shut up, and I'll point out to you all the famous people you've seen on telly but wouldn't recognize without their make-up – although,' whisper, 'let it be said straight away that a lot of them have got make-up on now. Amazing how they *will* keep forgetting the cold cream!'

It was a good job really that Andy was disposed to talk to her, for it was quite obvious that none of the others was: Sandra talked to the two girls, and looked over her shoulder every thirty seconds at the door, obviously expecting someone special, and Pete talked across Janet to Dave about something terribly technical to do, as far as she could gather, with lighting. Meanwhile, her self-appointed court jester indicated all the people he thought she ought to know with jabs of his long-nailed forefinger, and loud, and invariably rude, comments.

Despite herself, Janet was interested, and thought herself pretty lucky to get into company like this on her first evening in London. She had come here, after all, for excitement and change, and the inside of any world in the public eye was fascinating. She did recognize many of the people sitting and standing round the bar, and many more she knew by name from the credits of television programmes. Andy's rude comments were, though often quite unbelievable, rather amusing, and she found that she was enjoying herself, and her wish that Vicky were there was now from wanting her to share the fun rather than from needing her support.

Sandra's Sister Anne act at last had its reward: she looked over her shoulder for the umpteenth time, and suddenly smiled widely, turned in her seat and sat up straighter. Janet followed the direction of her eyes, and saw a tall, fairly good-looking young man, impeccably dressed in a biscuit-coloured suit and floral shirt and tie coming across from the door, and smiling in Sandra's direction. There was a general murmur of greeting for him from the group as a whole, and a special greeting from Sandra, who, moreover, introduced him to Janet with the same sort of proprietary pride as she had introduced Portobello Market.

'Richard, I'd like you to meet my new flat-mate from back home, Janet Anderson. Janet, this is Richard Murray.'

Janet by now had her wits about her, and the very way that Sandra said his name made her realize that she ought to have heard of him, so that, although it was not a programme she watched, she was able to say, 'How do you do? I've seen you on the television, of course, as Dr. Booth.'

'Have you?' he said, without much interest, but Janet was saved from feeling completely snubbed by Sandra's grateful smile. Dear me, these actor types were very touchy – she had always thought they were only annoyed if no-one noticed them. 'Sorry I'm late, Sandy, bit of a hold up.'

'I think it's just about my round,' Dave said, standing up and trying to edge his hand into the pocket of his very tight trousers. 'What'll you have, Dick?'

'Oh, are we staying here? I rather thought we'd be going out to a pub,' Richard said. The others looked at each other uncertainly.

'Well, I don't mind,' Dave said eventually.

'Of course you don't,' Andy told him, 'it means you miss your round.'

'Considering you haven't bought one all evening, I don't think you should talk,' Sue said sharply to Andy, who replied just as quickly, 'What a suburban mind you have, dear. Even primitive societies support their men of learning, the witch-doctors and wise men who don't contribute to the tribal food-reserves but are still just as essential ... however, since it worries you so, I will buy the first round in the next hostelry we stop at.'

'In that case,' said Pete, 'we must definitely go elsewhere. The sight of Andy buying a round is not to be missed.'

'Why don't we go to the "York"?' Richard suggested with

an air of just having thought of it, though Janet was sure he had intended it all along.

'Well, I don't mind where we go, as long as we go somewhere and stop wasting time talking about it,' said Sally irritably.

'All not in favour, say aye,' Andy said. 'The "York" let it be, then.' He turned his attention to Janet and explained, 'It's a pub much frequented by Beeb people and actors of various marks – I expect dear Richard wants to be seen.'

'What *do* you do?' Janet asked him, intrigued, as they walked towards the door at the head of their group.

'I'm an absolutely vital kind of person to have around. That's why I can be rude to all these actors with impunity.'

'Yes, but what —?'

'I'm a cameraman,' he told her.

'Oh,' said Janet. Somehow it was the last thing she would have thought of.

They made the short journey by car, Sue and Dave in Dave's Mini, Sally with Pete in his open Spitfire, and Andy, Janet, Sandra and Richard in the latter's Triumph saloon. During the drive Janet reflected that the cars were typical of their owners, just as it was typical of what she knew of Andy that he should not have one. After some difficulty they all managed to find somewhere to park, and walked along a narrow side-street to the pub. Some people were sitting outside at tables on the pavement, and the doors of the pub were open, giving a faintly continental air to the scene. It was crowded inside, but they pushed in anyway, and stood huddled together like cattle while Andy, reluctantly, and Pete, grimly, went up to the bar to get the drinks. Janet watched them worm their way in, and wondered how they would ever get back out without spilling whatever they bought. Sandra was in close conversation with Richard, whom Janet realized was her boyfriend, though he was looking around him instead of at her, and nodding and smiling to various people round the bar who knew him, or whom he knew, whichever it was.

'This place gets so horribly crowded nowadays,' Sally said crossly. 'All those beastly people from the drama school come pushing in here.'

'It's not them I mind,' said Sue, 'it's all those Irish round the other side. I don't know why they come in here – I wouldn't have thought it was their sort of pub at all.'

'They probably only come in here because they've been barred from all the other pubs in the area,' Sally said, and then hissed angrily as a woman, pushing past her towards the door, stepped on her foot. 'Clumsy idiot,' she muttered under her breath.

'Oh, look, those people in the corner are going. Let's get in quick,' Sue said.

'Thank God,' Sally breathed, and Janet silently agreed with her – perhaps it would put her in a better humour. There was room for four to sit down in the vacated corner. Sue and Sally dived in quickly, and Sandra sat down on the end of the seat, still talking to Richard, who stood beside her. Dave looked at Janet with raised eyebrows, offering the other place, but Janet refused hastily.

'Oh, no thanks, really, I'd rather stand.' Stuck in that corner with those two? That wouldn't be much of an amusing evening. Seeing Dave still hesitate, she said, 'I've been sitting down nearly all day on a train – I'd much rather stand.'

Dave shrugged and sat down, and Andy appeared at that moment bearing a tray with six of the drinks on it. Behind him, Pete, elbows in and hands up, holding two over-full pint mugs, was wriggling out from the crowd round the bar. He gave one pint to Dave, and seeing Sue and Sally were again deep in conversation with each other, engaged him in conversation. Andy began to talk shop with Richard, and since Sandra seemed to be in a deep dream of her own, Janet was left to look around the pub and think her own thoughts.

It was not like any of the pubs at home. There, young people only went into certain pubs, and then only the ones that had been altered especially for them and made into discos and that sort of thing. A pub like this, back home, would have been the haunt of the middle-aged and old; there certainly wouldn't be any happy mixture of ages as there was here. She felt she was going to like London after all, and already the society was an improvement on what she had had. True, Sue and Sally weren't particularly good company, but the others were all right, and she liked the look of the sort of people who were standing around her, and she liked the snatches of conversation she caught – why, no-one had yet even mentioned football, which was the only thing ever discussed at any length at home.

Richard was offering her a cigarette, and as she turned towards him to take it with a smile, she caught a glimpse of someone staring at her. Looking back, she saw a man standing by the door, a young man with dark smooth hair and very large blue eyes, whose face seemed vaguely familiar to Janet. He seemed to be staring at her as if he recognized her too, and wondering who it was she began tentatively to smile, when Richard's voice saying, 'Light, Janet?' called her attention away until she had lit her cigarette. When she looked back again, he had gone, presumably out of the door, and though she glanced in that direction from time to time during the evening, she did not see him again. He must have gone home, and since he didn't come across to speak to her, he couldn't have recognized her. Oh, of course! She was standing right next to Dr. Booth of Friday night fame – it was him that the stranger had recognized! How silly of her to think it was her. And yet, his face did seem familiar at the time. She wondered why.

CHAPTER FIVE

They got up very late on Sunday, and by the time they'd had breakfast and read the papers and yawned about idly and got themselves tidied up, it was past one o'clock. When Janet came back to the kitchen from washing herself, she found Sandra still sitting listlessly at the kitchen table picking at her nails.

'Isn't it late? What do you usually do on a Sunday?' Janet asked. She looked around and then decided that she might as well do the washing-up while they were talking.

'Depends,' Sandra said, and then making an effort she sat up a little and said, 'Sometimes we go down to the "Kensington" and listen to the jazz – that's if we don't get up too late and everyone isn't working. If the weather's nice we sometimes go out to Ruislip or Rickmansworth or somewhere for a swim. But I don't think anyone's doing anything in particular today.' She yawned and scratched the top of her head. 'Oh God,' she gaped half way through her yawn, 'I'll have to stop drinking gin.'

Janet laughed at that.

'You sound about forty. Really, when you say things like that, no-one would ever believe you're only the same age as me. In fact I'm a couple of months older than you. When's your birthday?'

'June.'

'There you are then. Mine's February.' She clashed two dinner plates in the washing-up bowl, and Sandra winced theatrically.

'Don't bang about like that. You may be older in actual time, but I've lived far more than you, I'm older in feeling. You don't know how lucky you are, living a sheltered life back home, protected and looked after. London puts years on you.'

'Come off it. You chose to come here, and you chose to stay here. I don't believe you regret a minute of it. And if you do,

46

more fool you. You could always go home.'

'It's positively obscene to be as cheerful as that first thing in the morning,' Sandra said with dignity, dragging herself up. 'I think I'll go back to bed and read.' She got as far as the door, and then turned back and said, 'By the way, I'm going out with Richard tonight, so you'll be left to your own resources.'

'O.K.,' Janet said cheerfully. 'I'll manage.'

She finished the washing-up and tidied the kitchen, and then sat down to consider what to do. She was not as cheerful as she had sounded, for she discovered she had banked on Sandra's leadership and company to get her through the first few days. Of course, she shouldn't have. Sandra had every right to go out with her own boy-friend – it would be ridiculous if she put him off for her, Janet's, sake. However, it did leave her rather at a loose end.

She gave herself a shaking and talked to herself in Vicky's voice. Nonsense, girl! You must be soft, goin' on like that! The whole of London at your mercy, and you sit indoors cringing like a ninny. Janet smiled and answered herself. Quite right. I'm going to put my coat on right now and go out and see what I can find going on.

She slipped on a short corduroy jacket, ran a brush through her hair, letting it hang loose as it would, and then calling to Sandra that she was going out for a walk, she let herself out and ran down the stairs to the street. It was warm and sunny, though still a little muggy and damp, but on the whole a nice day for a walk. There was the usual litter of prams and tricycles in the hallway, and a bunch of kids were sitting on the front steps, presumably playing mothers, since two of them held dolls carefully in their arms, and one of them held a battered teddy wrapped in a piece of ironing blanket, and yet another had arranged her arms in the right position for carrying a baby, even though the arms were empty.

'Excuse me,' Janet said politely as she climbed over them, but they did not answer, only stared up at her with their mouths open. They'd probably never heard those words before, Janet thought. She walked along the road towards the main road, and noticed with amusement how about one in two

47

of all the people in sight were washing cars. Plastic buckets of all hues blossomed on the pavements, and the gutters ran with white glittering suds. It was such an odd contrast, the snotty-nosed kids and peeling, neglected houses on the one hand, and the glossy, freshly-laundered cars on the other. She turned up towards the station, heading in the direction of a loud clattering noise of road-works. There seemed to be a lot of people around, far more than there would be at home on a Sunday, where everyone was either indoors having their Sunday dinner at this time or had gone in cars and buses to visit relations in the outer districts. A lot of these people seemed to be walking dogs, and she saw lots of Afghans and Borzois, several Alsatians, and a Great Dane, but the most popular breed of all still seemed to be the golden retriever.

The people who were parading the streets all seemed to be very smart; even those who were untidy were untidy in a smart, fashionable sort of way. Most of the women wore trousers, which made her glad she had come out in a pair of cord jeans, and lots of beads. The men's favourite garb seemed to be velvet trousers and thin cheesecloth shirts open, well open, at the front. The sight of so many hairy chests, she said to herself, is enough to put one off one's dinner.

Portobello Road was lively, with all the junk and antique stalls out, but Janet missed the loud continuous banter of the fruit and veg. merchants. The antique merchants stood silently by their stalls, looking sullen and smoking endless cigarettes. There were a lot of people here who were smart in a different sort of way, and these were obviously the intruders from another, richer part of London, trying to pick up a bargain. You could tell them by their tidy hairstyles and their neat coats; the women by their shoes. Janet wandered along the line of stalls, and now and then stopped to turn over the goods idly. It mostly was junk, and a lot of it not even old. There were several stalls selling those cheap bangles and rings that the tout sold outside the station in her home town, from a suitcase.

She had passed the shopping part now, and seemed to be in a purely residential part of the street. This was not so interesting, and she thought of turning back, but she noticed that the road narrowed and turned a corner, so she decided to go as far as the corner at least, to see what it was like. The little houses here had all been well kept and painted up, so different from the house she lived in now; and there on the corner was a dear little pub, flower bowls and leaded windows and all! And what a nice name, 'The Sun in Splendour'. One of the bar doors was open, and a cheerful noise came from it. She glanced at her watch – a quarter to two. She would have liked to go in there, but she didn't like to go into a pub on her own – it didn't seem right somehow. Oh, come now, she admonished herself. This is London – nobody minds what you do in London. And how are you going to have any adventures if you're scared even to walk into a pub at your advanced age.

She screwed up her courage and walked in at the door, but the sensation that all eyes were upon her stopped her, and she looked around ostentatiously as if she were scanning the bar for somebody she expected to be there. To her enormous surprise she immediately recognized somebody, and with a mixture of relief and annoyance she returned the smile and nod she received from Andy, who was standing with his back to the bar and leaning on it with his elbows. He beckoned her across with a skinny forefinger, and she had no choice really but to go.

'Well if it isn't Miss Leeds! What brings you to this haunt of vice on the Sabbath? Drinking alone on a Sunday lunchtime is the first step to becoming an alcoholic, you know.'

'Well, I wasn't actually,' Janet began, feeling rather foolish, and then stopped. She had been going to say that she wasn't here to drink, but what else could she be here for? Besides, it had been her first intention.

'Wasn't actually what?' Andy asked, smiling at her confusion. 'You should cultivate that blush, by the way. It's very attractive.'

'Is it?' Janet said faintly.

'Certainly. There are very few girls who can blush nowadays. What can I get you to drink?'

'Can I have a half of lager?' Janet asked.

'Draught? Yes, certainly,' and he turned his back to her for a moment to order it, with much banter, from the barmaid

49

whom he apparently knew well.

'Are you drinking alone here?' Janet asked when he turned back again.

'That rather depends,' Andy replied, smiling archly, 'on what you mean by alone. If you mean, did I come in with anyone, no, I didn't. But I am a great favourite with all the barstaff here – I come to drink with them.'

'How do you come to know them?' Janet asked, feeling the need to keep up the conversation.

'I know all the barmen and barmaids in this district. Being a regular in most of the pubs round here, and being a connoisseur of a good pint, I naturally get to know the people who serve me. I am of a gregarious nature. That means talkative,' he added in a tone that was very nearly normal. Despite herself, Janet found herself liking him. She felt rather sorry for him, that he was a lone drinker, and had to rely on barmaids for company, and sorry for him that he had to bolster up his own confidence so obviously. But he was rather amusing.

'You haven't answered me yet,' Andy said, handing her her half pint. 'What are you doing here?'

'Well, I was out for a walk, exploring y'might say, and I saw this pub and thought it looked rather pretty, so I just came to the door to look round and see if it was as nice inside, and then I spotted you.'

'I see. So you had no impure thoughts of drinking alcohol, until I tempted you, and you fell?'

'You might say that,' Janet laughed.

'I did,' Andy said solemnly. 'And why has your hostess left you to your own devices on your first Sunday in London? Don't you think that's unkind?'

'I think she had a headache or something – anyway, she went back to bed. I don't suppose she thinks of herself as a hostess – after all, I'm supposed to be a flat-mate only, and you don't expect to have to hold flat-mate's hands for them, do you? I wouldn't have expected her to tag me along with her all the time.'

Andy narrowed his eyes and stared at her while she was talking, and when she stopped he said, 'I'll tell you about you – you're a nice girl, with a kind, forgiving heart. You think

50

that our lovely Sandy should have looked after you, and you have said to yourself that you would have done so if she had been the newcomer and you were in her position. But you would never say so to anyone else, and you're so ready to forgive her you don't even know you're doing it.'

Janet felt herself blushing again, to her annoyance, and buried her nose in her beer to hide her face. Unfortunately she gulped a bit too fast, and nearly choked, which only made her embarrassment worse. Andy took her glass out of her hand so that she could cough in peace without spilling, and by the time she recovered, breathless and watery-eyed, he was nearly helpless with laughter. For a moment she was ready to be annoyed, but after a while she couldn't help laughing too, and after that the ice was well and truly broken between them, and there was no more awkwardness.

'Oh you are priceless,' Andy said at last, on the tail end of his giggles. 'Here, take your glass back, I must blow my nose.'

'Can I ask you something?' Janet said when he was visible again from behind his man-sized Kleenex.

'Anything,' he said obligingly.

'Have you got Chinese parents, or something? Sometimes you look very Chinese.' She glanced at him doubtfully and added, 'I hope you don't think I'm very rude, asking.'

'I forgive you,' he said, smiling. 'Actually, my father's father was Chinese – and his mother was German, so I've got a very villainous background. Many's the girl that's disappeared shortly after being seen talking to me on a street corner in Soho.'

'I'll risk it,' Janet smiled.

'You're remarkably difficult to frighten,' Andy complained. 'You spoil all my best lines.'

'I suppose it must be catching, working with actors all the time,' Janet said. 'In the end you're bound to talk as if you're reading a script.'

'So that's what you think of me!' Andy said, pretending outrage. 'Well now, for that insult, you'll have to answer me a question in payment.'

'Fire away,' Janet said. 'I've nothing to hide.'

'All right then, and you must answer honestly. Why did you

come to London? Was it to seek adventure, to see the lights, to make your fortune? Excitement and glamour?'

Janet smiled.

'You make it sound so silly,' she said.

'You must tell the truth,' he reminded her.

'Well then, it was. I was bored stiff with life at home, nothing to do, no new faces, no prospects. I thought London couldn't be worse and might even be better.'

'There's a good girl, you've admitted it,' Andy said, looking pleased. 'Well, there's no reason to be ashamed of that. The only thing you need be ashamed of is failure. It's lucky really that you happened to have Sandra for your contact.'

'Why?'

'Because she introduced you to me, and I can introduce you to a lot of interesting people. It won't be my fault if you don't find life a bit more exciting here than in – wherever it is.'

'Thanks very much,' Janet said, fighting the urge to ask why he would be doing all this for a complete stranger, because it was a gauche sort of question, and would look like fishing for compliments.

'Not at all. Don't mention it. And we'll start this very evening. You will come along with me to the studios, and watch us filming the latest episode of "The Redding Family". How about that?'

'I'd really like that,' Janet said, pleased. 'Can I really come? I mean, you can get me in all right?'

'Sweetie,' Andy said, 'I'm a cameraman. That's only one step down from God.'

Whether Andy's estimate of his own importance was right or not, there was certainly no difficulty in getting her in. Andy picked her up at the flat at five, and they went by bus to Shepherd's Bush Green, and then walked through some back streets to the back entrance of the building she was in before. There was a commissionaire on the gate but he didn't even glance at them as they walked past, up the sloping private road, and in through a covered area where a telephone booth stood propped up against the wall next to a bundle of road-signs. Andy ushered her down a long corridor and through some swing doors, and she found herself at last in a real TV studio. The first thing she noticed was the lights. The room was huge, like an aircraft hangar, but the whole ceiling was covered in lights, some large, some small, some apparently fixed, others on rails, moveable. Every inch had its light, it seemed, and with the black-painted iron rails that they were fixed on, and the flex and brackets and shutters, it looked like an electrician's nightmare, an absolute jungle.

She looked around, fascinated. There were four cameras, light grey in colour, with a little red light on top, each with a seat attached so that it was like one of those electric trolleys that are driven around railway stations. Two of them were occupied already, and were being shifted backwards and forwards while their drivers looked into the eye piece and twiddled.

'That's my beauty over there,' Andy said, pointing to one of the unoccupied cameras. 'Number three.'

'What's the light on top for?' Janet asked.

'It lights up when the picture being taken is selected in the control room – that's up there, look. And there, and there, are monitor screens – that will show you what *is* being selected at any time. I have to go and have a word over there. Stay here, don't worry, no-one will throw you out. If anyone asks what you're doing, say Andy Lam brought you.'

He dashed off towards a group of people holding some kind of argument and waving clipboards about to emphasize their points. Janet continued to look round at the multitude of people, trying to decide what the job of each was. The only ones she could really be sure of were those still engaged in fixing up the sets. There were two, one being the Edwardian-style sitting room that was already familiar to her from having watched 'The Redding Family' on television, and the other a bedroom of the same period. Each was absolutely perfect except that it only had three walls. It was astonishing to see them open on one side like that, for, however much one knew that they were only sets, when you saw the finished programme on TV you always saw them as whole, proper rooms.

She saw one of the cameras slide silently forward and its little red light came on. She glanced up at the monitor nearest

53

her and saw the familiar sitting room, complete and convincing, glanced down and saw it made of wood and open to the world on one side. The comparison amused her and she looked from one to the other and back again until the picture went off.

Andy came back to her.

'We'll be starting in about ten minutes. I have to get ready, so I'll have to leave you. Find yourself a chair where you can see properly. Look, there are Sir John and Lady Redding – over there, see? I must go. See you later.'

Janet, preoccupied with staring around, and particularly at the two costumed actors who had just come in, scarcely noticed he had gone, until he came into her line of sight again, this time seated at his camera, and wearing a huge pair of padded earphones like a pilot's. He looked very impressive, very capable, almost awesome as he consulted his clipboard, moved his seat up and down, turned his head towards the glass front of the control room and made a rapid series of gestures with one hand which evidently had a coded meaning. She mused on how he behaved like an ass socially, while his job was so important, and he was so obviously a highly qualified man.

A little while later the actors and some of the important-looking people who had been arguing earlier drifted over to the bedroom set and it was evident that the action was going to begin. After more discussion the two actors took up their positions and waited while the lights were adjusted and the long microphone boom was hoisted an inch or two until it disappeared off the monitored picture. Then someone shouted that they were going to begin, and a hush fell. For a moment the actors remained ordinary people, staring out of the brightly lit set for a signal, and then suddenly they were Sir John and Lady Redding having a very refined argument in their bedroom. It went on for a few minutes, and then someone shouted something, and instantly they were actors again, the bedroom a set, and the woman very carefully inserted a fingernail into her piled-up hair to scratch an itch on her scalp in a disarmingly human way.

Janet was enthralled. As the filming went on and she saw that movement in the studio was not forbidden, she moved

54

around, keeping well to the back out of everyone's way, so that she could view things from different angles and eavesdrop on snatches of technical conversation, finding out what jobs other people did around the studio. No-one seemed to notice her, certainly no-one suggested even by a slight frown that she shouldn't be there, so she was quite happy.

After about an hour the man who had started everything off shouted, 'All right, break for ten minutes' and disappeared in the direction of the control room. The lights in the back part of the studio came on, and everyone relaxed into conversation. The actors came off the set and wandered across to join a group, and cups of tea began to appear. Janet saw Andy talking to someone and looking across in her direction. In a moment the young man he had been talking to came across to her and said,

'Are you Janet? Andy can't leave his camera, so he said I was to get you a cup of tea and talk to you. D'you want to come with me to the canteen?'

'Yes, O.K.,' Janet said. She was fighting the idea in her brain that she wanted to go to the toilet, but fighting in vain. It was no use. As they went through the swing doors, she said to her companion, 'I say, is there a ladies' anywhere near?'

'Oh, er – let me think.' He stopped and looked up and down the corridor. 'Yes, there's one that way – follow the corridor, and it's about eight rooms down.'

Janet glanced down the corridor, and doubtfully back at the door of the studio. Would she find her way back again? All the doors looked the same to her. The young man saw her look and said kindly, 'I'll wait for you outside this door if you like. I should be back with the tea before you're back with – I mean, before you've finished.' He stopped, looking thoroughly confused, which put Janet at ease.

'Thanks,' she said, and darted off in the direction he had showed her.

Back in the studio, sipping her tea and gratefully relieved, she asked the young man, whose name was Don, and who said he was an electrician, lots of questions, which he seemed pleased to answer. That was the producer, and over there, that was the script writer. Continuity? Those two girls over there, talking to the man with glasses – he was the assistant producer. Andy? Yes, he was one of the best cameramen in the business. Could have made a big name for himself in films if he'd wanted – no, not as an actor, as a cameraman, of course.

Feeling rather foolish for having asked the last question, Janet was silent a while, and then the assistant stage manager clapped his hands loudly and the lights at the back were dimmed again, and the work started anew. The business now was more complicated as there were several exits and entrances to manage, and four characters on the set at once. Janet was getting involved in the story now, managing to follow it through the stops and starts, and she became quite oblivious to her surroundings until some time later, when a pause for the make-up girl to run on and powder out a sweat-shine on Lady Redding's forehead left Janet's attention free for a moment, and she became aware of the crawly sensation down her back that she always got when someone was looking at her.

She turned around and looked. Over by the swing doors, almost directly behind her, was a group of people, but it was quite dark there, and she had been staring at the brightly-lit set, and her eyes did not adjust that quickly – she could see nothing clearly. She looked away, and fixed her eyes on another dimly-lit part of the studio until they had adjusted and then looked back – two complete strangers stood by the door, neither of them looking at her. But the door was swinging gently, as if someone had just gone out, and she was sure that there had been more than two people there before. Ah well, probably she had been mistaken, no-one had been looking at her. In any case, she'd certainly never know now.

They finished for the evening at nine o'clock, and Janet was surprised at how punctually on the hour they stopped, thinking that it would be like the theatre where nothing ever went to plan or ran on time. Andy took her upstairs to the bar for a drink as soon as he was ready, and when she mentioned this to him he laughed and said they couldn't afford to be like that in television, when there was so much going on at the same time, and so many people wanting to use the same studios and the same equipment.

'Remember,' he said, 'there are still a lot of live programmes, and if the recorded ones ran over time, it might hold up a live one that was going out from the same studio. Apart from that, all the programmes run on a budget, and wages are practically the most expensive item.'

Janet nodded in appreciation of the fact. She was beginning to feel at home now, and when they arrived at the top floor and went into the bar, she thought she saw a flicker of recognition in the doorman's eye.

The bar was quite crowded, and Janet stuck close by Andy as he went up to order their drinks. She recognized a few people who had been in there last night; one of them greeted Andy with a wave, and gave her a nod too.

'Here you are. Cheers,' Andy said, handing her a drink.

'Thanks. And thank you, too, for letting me come along. I've really enjoyed it. It was exciting.'

'Not at all. But if you really want excitement, you should come when we're doing a live show. Why don't you come on Tuesday afternoon – we've a quiz show. You might like that.'

Janet hesitated.

'I'd like to, but —'

'But what?' Andy said, almost impatiently.

'Well, I've got to get a job. I can't live on my savings for ever, and I expect I'll have to take an office job, which means I might not still be free on Tuesday.'

'You sound very glum at the thought.'

'I am. I hate the idea of working in an office. I did it at home, and I really wanted a change, but I'm not really qualified for anything else.'

'What do you do, then?'

'I'm a machine operator. You know, Burroughs and that sort of thing.'

'Why don't you come and work at the Beeb? Everyone does, sooner or later. They must need Burroughs-women, whatever they may be.'

'Well, I suppose that would be better than an accounts office, but —'

'But what? You must make it a rule to finish your sentences. It's a very annoying habit, ending everything with "but".'

Janet smiled.

'All right, point taken. What I should have said is, it wouldn't really be all that much of a change, it would still be working in an office. I want to meet people, and have a bit of fun. Offices are all much the same, and machinists are so often shut away by themselves.'

'I see your point.' Andy pondered for a moment, and then his face brightened. 'I say, I've just had a stroke of absolute genius. The answer to your prayers. I can get you fixed up in a job where you'll meet new people all the time, plenty of opportunity to chat, time off during the day, handy to your home, and as much booze as you can drink.'

'What is it?' Janet asked, interested.

'Barmaid. Up at the "York". Friend of mine who works at the "Sun" told me they've been a barmaid short for weeks. I'm well known in there. A word from me, and the job's yours.' Janet was silent, wondering whether he did have that much influence, and wondering even more if she would like being a barmaid. 'Well, what do you say?' Andy urged her.

'I don't know. I've never been a barmaid. I wouldn't know how.'

'Everyone has a first time. A bright girl like you would pick it up in no time.'

'But wouldn't they be wanting someone with experience?'

'No, don't you worry about that. Pubs like that are always taking on beginners and training them. It takes so little time to pick up that no-one worries about lack of experience.' Janet still hesitated. 'Come on, what's the worry? It's a nice job, easy. Lean on the bar all lunchtime chatting to the regulars. Plenty of tips. Get to know all the famous people of Notting Hill Gate. You can't say it isn't a change from an office.'

'Do you really think I'd get the job, though?'

'My dear girl, it's already yours,' Andy said largely.

'All right then, thanks. I'll give it a try,' Janet said, and at that moment she got the shivery feeling again that someone was looking at her, and she shuddered and glanced round behind her.

'Good girl,' Andy was saying, and then seeing her shiver, said, 'What's up?'

'Ghost walking on my grave, that's all,' she said. There was no-one that she could see looking at her, but she had the impression of someone tall and dark-haired going out of the swing doors of the bar just as she turned round – she had barely caught a glimpse, so it could not be more than an impression, but it unnerved her. I'm being haunted by swing doors, she thought.

'I'll call for you tomorrow morning, about eleven, and we'll go in and see the boss and fix you up,' Andy said.

'Thanks. I hope I'm not putting you to any trouble,' Janet murmured conventionally.

'Of course you're not,' Andy said. 'I'm putting myself to it.'

CHAPTER SIX

At lunchtime the pub was quieter, and most of the people there were sitting at tables reading newspapers and eating sandwiches. There was a peaceful, relaxed air about the place; the sun came in through the high windows in broad beams through which the dust motes fell slowly and endlessly, and the few people who were speaking did so in hushed voices, as if they were in church.

Andy rather changed that by bouncing in at the door with a cheerful 'Wotcher, Mary!' to the black-haired barmaid behind the bar, and turning to Janet said, 'Usual?' and without waiting for an answer said to the barmaid, 'Half of lager and a dry martini, please darling. Is Stan around?'

'He's in the back having his cup of coffee, love,' the barmaid said comfortably, reaching under the counter for a glass. 'Do you want me to call him for you?'

'In a minute, Mary love. Let's have a drink first. This is Janet, by the way, a friend of mine. Janet – Mary, Ireland's finest flower, a sad loss to Ballyjamesduff.'

'Pay no attention to him,' Mary said to Janet with a wink. She had very little Irish accent – just a faint trace now and again. 'As if he didn't know I'm from Cork.'

'How would I know that? You're a dark horse, Mary my love. You never tell anyone anything about yourself.'

'Oh, Jasusnow, you could tell that for yourself from my talking,' Mary said with a parody of an accent. She slapped the half-pint mug down on the counter, spun round on the spot, taking a glass down from the shelf all in the same movement, pressed the glass up against the bar of the patent-measurer on the bottle neck, and a moment later completed her turn on the spot and put the glass down in front of Andy. Janet, who, like most people, had never watched a barmaid with any attention, was impressed now by the efficiency of this one, and especially by the economy of movement. Would she

60

ever be able to do that? She doubted it.

'Thirty-one please – thank you. Will I go and call Stan for you now?'

'Oh, yes, thanks Mary. If he's still drinking his coffee, just say I'd like a word when he's finished. I'll be here a little while.'

'O.K.' And the handsome, black-haired woman disappeared through the doorway at the end of the bar.

Andy and Janet sipped their drinks for a while, then Andy glanced down at her and said, 'Nervous? You're looking a bit pale.' Janet nodded. 'You shouldn't be. Stan'll take you on, for my sake if not for yours. You'll be a great success. You've got all the qualifications.'

'What qualifications does a barmaid have to have?' Janet wanted to know.

'A big bosom and long arms,' Andy said with an absolutely straight face. 'Ah, there's Stan now. You stay here, and I'll go round and talk to him in the other bar. Less embarrassing all round if you're not there to hear us discussing you.'

Janet saw the tall, portly man come round from the other side of the horse-shoe-shaped bar, and Andy went to meet him and took him back round, out of Janet's sight, talking hard. Janet swallowed nervously and took another sip of beer. Mary re-emerged from the back and picking up a tea-cloth began to wipe glasses and put them back on the shelves and on the high rack over the bar-top. Janet could see now why Andy had said 'long arms'.

In a very little time Andy came back, with Stan at his shoulder.

'Janet, meet Stan, the Guv'nor.' He was a tall, heavy man with a florid face and a very stern, military bearing which gave everyone the impression that he wore a bristling moustache, though in fact he was clean-shaven. He looked at Janet from under his eyebrows and she felt exactly as if the headmaster had spotted her talking in prayers, but when she steeled herself to meet his eye, she saw that his eyes were friendly, humorous.

'So, you want to be a barmaid, eh?' he asked her loudly. She felt as if she should say, yes, please sir, and I'm sorry, but instead she smiled and nodded to him. 'When can you start?'

61

was his next question, which rather took Janet aback, as she hadn't expected to be accepted so quickly.

'Anytime,' she said. 'Tomorrow, if you like.'

'Tomorrow morning. Come at half past ten – to this door. Knock on it and I'll let you in. All right?'

'Yes, er – thanks,' Janet said. She wanted to ask what the wages were, but she didn't like to bring the subject of money up – it was a more embarrassing topic nowadays than sex.

'Don't you want to know anything else?' Stan asked, much amused by her dumbness.

'Well I would like to know – er, what hours I have to work.'

'Eleven sessions a week. I'll pay you thirty bob a session for the first week, and if you make out all right I'll pay you two pound. And your tips are your own, of course. O.K.? Right, I'll see you tomorrow at ten-thirty. Don't be late. Must go now, work to do. I've got no cellarman, you know.'

'What happened to Liam?' Andy asked in surprise.

'Went back to Ireland. Can't think why. He won't get the same sort of wages over there. Still, that's the Irish for you – spend all their youth saving to come to England, then spend their time over here longing to get back and getting drunk from homesickness.' He gave a comical snort, lifted a hand in valediction, and strode away, out to the back.

'He loves them really,' Andy said. 'Otherwise why would he have a ninety per cent Irish staff? Want another drink?'

'Yes, but not here,' Janet said. 'Now I'm practically on the staff, I feel a bit shy of sitting here drinking.'

'O.K., we'll go down to the "Hoop", and I'll introduce you to the barman there – the sooner you get to know your fellow-sufferers the better. You never know when you'll need help from them.'

At exactly ten-thirty on Tuesday Janet arrived at the door of the pub wearing a thin, short-sleeved red jumper, a black skirt and flat shoes – all of which had taken her half an hour to decide on. Sandra had refused to have anything to do with the choosing at first, having given it as her opinion the evening before that Janet wanted her head looking at, taking on a job like that which everyone knew was only done full-time by the lowest of the low. It was all right, in her opinion, to be a temporary part-time evening barmaid at a smart pub when you needed more money, but to be a full-time barmaid —! Well, if Janet wanted her opinion, she wouldn't tell them at home what she was doing for a living or her father would be down on the first train to fetch her back.

Janet was surprised at such violently old-fashioned views from a self-styled swinger, but having accepted them she was not surprised when her appeal for help over the choice of clothes the next morning was met with a 'Don't ask me! I wash my hands of you.' Clothes, however, were Sandra's reigning passion, and it wasn't more than a few minutes before she wandered into Janet's room, where the latter was anxiously turning over her entire wardrobe, and said, 'You've got to be careful what you wear, y'know. You've got to be smart, but not too glamorous. And you've to remember that you'll probably get beer all down whatever it is, so it'd better be something easy to wash.' And with that she forgot her scruples and flung herself into the solving of the problem with right good will.

So here she was outside the pub. As Janet put her hand up to knock on the glass of the door, it was opened from inside and she saw Stan there, beaming down at her with an open friendliness that surprised her.

'I saw you coming. You're nice and punctual I see. Well done.'

Janet followed him in, and he locked the door behind her with one of an enormous bunch of keys. The lights over the bar were on, but the others were not, which made the place rather gloomy. Apart from that all the ashtrays were still full, the floor was covered in dog-ends, there was a cluster of dirty glasses standing on one end of the counter, and the place had a horrid smell – a mixture of old beer and cold cigarette reek. It was an unaccustomed smell, and it made Janet wrinkle up her nose in disgust, though she very soon got used to it and no longer noticed it, except when she first came in in the mornings – and even then, it did not smell so bad to her ever again as on that first morning.

Stan took her behind the bar, pushed a duster into her hand, and said, 'Dust the glass shelves, and just have a look round, find out where things are, that sort of idea. Most of the bottled beers are priced, and the draught prices are stuck up by the mirror there. I'm afraid I can't stand and hold your hand – I've got to bottle up. Mary should be here soon – she'll tell you anything you want to know.'

With that he left her and went out the back. Janet began to dust the shelves, which was tedious since they were all covered in knick-knacks, little souvenirs, plastic flowers in red-glass vases, miniatures, a pewter mug half full of coins. They obviously hadn't been dusted for a long time, for when she lifted the bits and pieces off, they left clean circles in the dust. While she did this, she stared hard all around her and tried to memorize where everything was. Guinness, Mackeson, cider. Worthington, light ale, brown ale, more Guinness. Half-pint mugs there, pint mugs there. Three different sizes of stem glasses. Why? she wondered. The view of the pub from the bar was strange and made her feel most peculiar. The view of the inside of the bar was new too, and everything looked raw and unfinished, with the metal sinks and draining boards, and the Formica surfaces with circular stains on them where the wet glasses had stood mouth down.

There were some dark-grey, bedraggled-looking dish-cloths lying in the sink – surely they didn't wash up with those? – and on every available surface tea-cloths had been stretched out the night before to dry. These little woggly things were what you took the tops off bottles with, she supposed. Now, could she remember where things were? She shut her eyes and tried to visualize. Guinness, Mackeson, cider. What next? Oh God, she would never be able to find anything when asked.

Up there were the bottles of spirits, upside down with their patent measures in their necks. Whisky, gin, vodka, whisky, gin, rum, brandy. The brandy was nearly empty. Borrowing trouble she visualized herself having to serve brandy and only getting half a glassful out. What would she do then?

The beer pumps, she saw, were just like ordinary taps. That was a relief in a way, though also a slight disappointment, for she had had an image of herself flexing her arm in a professional way and drawing off a perfect pint. She loved to have

64

unusual skills. Better finish those shelves off quick, before any-one came in.

She had dusted all the glass shelves and was standing desperately staring at the bins full of bottles, trying to memorize position and price, when Mary came in from the back looking calm and pleasant, and, to Janet, remarkably like a rescue team.

'Hello, love! You joining us this side?'

'Yes – I was just trying to learn the prices —' Janet said, to excuse the fact that she was apparently doing nothing.

'Oh, don't worry about that. You'll pick them up as you go along. I wouldn't bother trying to learn them that way – you'll forget them again as soon.'

She bent and pushed her handbag behind some bottles in one of the bottom bins, looked in the mirror to settle her hair, and then looked around to see what needed doing.

'That Ernie hasn't swept the floor as usual,' she remarked. She looked at Janet who raised her eyebrows politely. 'He's an old feller who pots for us. S'posed to sweep out and wipe the tables, but forgets as often as not.'

'Shall I sweep it now?' Janet asked eagerly, anxious to prove her worth.

'If you like, love,' Mary said comfortably. Janet soon found she said that to almost any suggestion, peacefully indifferent as to who did the work, so long as it got done. 'The broom's out the back – here, I'll show you.'

Through the door into the passage beyond, and there was a bucket and mop, a broom and dustpan, some huge plastic containers on wheels, into which, Mary said, they threw the non-returnable bottles, and several stacks of crates, empty ones, for the returnable bottles. Janet took the broom and energetically swept the bar floor, while Mary pottered about behind the bar, taking the tea towels down, washing up the dirty glasses, emptying the ashtrays.

When she had all but finished, Stan came in with his sleeves rolled up, carrying the till drawers. He nodded at Janet and said, 'All right?' as he passed. Janet wanted to ask him what to do with the sweepings, but he shot past her too quickly, so she waited until he had put the drawers in the tills and left, and then asked Mary.

'Oh, give it to me, love. I'll take it – I've got to go down anyway, to see if Stan's turned on.' She took the broom and dustpan from Janet's hand and went away. Like characters in a farce, as she went out at one end of the bar, Stan came in at the other, carrying his bunch of keys, and unlocked the bar doors, and then went out again without even a glance at Janet. She began to feel very spare, but hoped that Mary would come back soon, because now it was opening time, and someone might come in, and she didn't know what to do. She picked up a drying cloth and dried the few glasses that Mary had washed, and looked at the door from time to time out of the corner of her eye, with the absurd feeling that looking at it directly would make a customer come in.

It happened. The door swung open, and a tall man in a raincoat and a trilby hat came in, sat down on a bar stool, opened his newspaper, and without looking at Janet said 'Pint of Special, please.'

Panic seized her. What was 'Special'? She moved slowly away from him, buying time. One of the illuminated pump tops said 'Special Bitter' – that must be it. Relief surged through her, and light-heartedly she picked up a pint mug, held it under the nozzle, and turned the tap. In one second flat the mug was filled with foam and it was pouring over the sides and on to the floor. She turned it off quickly and gulped with dismay. Obviously there was more to pouring a pint than just turning the tap. She glanced at the man, but he was reading his paper, apparently unaware of her situation. She stared desperately at the beer mug full of foam. What was she to do now? Wait till it subsided? But it didn't look as if it would subside for hours. Try another tap? But then she might get told off for wasting this one. She stood staring at the froth as if willing it to change into beer, and then Mary came in.

Janet gazed at her with huge relief, and whispered,

'It's come out all frothy. What do I do now?'

'Oh, that's all right – I've only just turned the pumps on. I haven't drawn it off yet. It'll be a minute or so before they settle down.'

It wasn't her fault, then. She was glad of that. But she had to go and tell the man he couldn't have his beer yet. He might be angry with her. Screwing up her courage she went back to where he sat at the bar, reading still, and said,

'I'm afraid the beer's only just been turned on. It'll be a minute or two —'

'Yes, all right,' the man said matter-of-factly, without looking up. Relief again – he hadn't shouted at her. She went back to watch Mary as the latter removed the little plastic trays from under the taps and emptied them into a big galvanized bucket, and then, holding the bucket high up under each tap in turn, ran off the foam from each.

'They'll be a bit high at first,' Mary told Janet, 'but if you pour them slowly and hold the glasses well tilted you'll be all right.'

'Yes, I see,' Janet said meekly, though she didn't know what 'a bit high' meant. Her tone of voice must have attracted Mary's notice, for she glanced up, and smiled at Janet kindly.

'Don't be looking so miserable. You'll feel a bit strange at first, but you'll soon get used to everything. Just take your time. Don't let anyone hurry you – we won't be busy this morning.'

Janet smiled her gratitude, and watched as Mary poured a pint of the Special and took it to the customer.

'There you are, colonel. Pint of the best.'

'Thanks, Mary,' the man said, pushing further forward the coins he had laid out ready on the counter, and then glanced across at Janet. 'Training the young entry, eh?'

'Yes, this is Janet, who's started with us this morning. This is the colonel, one of our old faithfuls.'

The man gave her a small, tight smile and a nod.

'Mary'll teach you right,' he said, and then reaching into his pocket and holding out a pound note, 'I'll have twenty Rothmans, please young lady.'

Janet took the pound note and looked towards Mary.

'Just round the corner, at the top,' she whispered discreetly, and added in a louder tone, 'Cigarette money goes in this till. All cigarette money in this till, everything else in either of the others.'

'O.K.,' Janet said more cheerfully, and did her task.

The morning passed slowly at first, for there were not many customers, and those Mary mostly served. She met Mrs. Wood, Stan's wife, who made and served the sandwiches at the end of the bar, served two people with pints and three with light ales (finding that getting the tops off the bottles required a particular sort of flexing of the wrist – the first one she tried, to her anguish, the bottle-neck shattered) and learnt what a whisky-mac was.

When one o'clock came, Stan told her to go for her coffee break, and showed her the little rest-room upstairs, and Mrs. Wood gave her a cup of coffee and offered her a sandwich, which she refused. She had nothing to do up there, and would really have preferred to be back downstairs in the bar where she could talk to Mary, but having been sat down in the rest-room, she felt obliged to sit there for the prescribed ten minutes before making her way downstairs again. When she arrived back in the bar she saw that it had got busy in the time she was away, and Stan was serving as well as Mary.

'All right, Mary,' Stan said when he saw Janet come hesitantly back in behind the counter, 'you can go off now. Tell Mrs. Wood I might have to call for her.'

Janet was not too pleased with the idea of being left at the bar with the boss, for she was very slow and uncertain, and had to ask the price of everything, and she didn't want to show Stan what a complete dummy she was. Then, to cap it all, the door opened and in walked Andy, with Dave behind him.

'There you are!' he exclaimed in his penetrating voice. Several people looked at him, and then looked at Janet to see what the fuss was about. 'The answer to a young man's prayers. The dream barmaid of all time, lovely and languorous. I told everyone, and they're all coming in to see you pull pints.'

'Hello, Andy,' Janet said in a subdued voice, aware that Stan was staring at her and feeling sure that it was in disapproval. 'Hello Dave. What can I get you?'

'Sweet words! Music to my ears. I'll have a dry martini, and Dave here will have – what?'

'Light and bitter,' Dave said, watching Janet unsmilingly. Inwardly cursing them she went over to Stan, and blushing

68

with chagrin, asked him how one did a dry martini and a light and bitter. Stan did not frown at her, or laugh at her; in fact, he seemed strangely pleased, as if her ignorance were something good about her.

'Dry martini's in a bottle – there, look – and you fill the double measure – yes, that's the one – and put it in one of those glasses. Light and bitter, you half fill a pint mug with Special, uncap a light ale, and let him pour it.'

'How far is half full?' Janet asked, even more timidly, hating to have to ask everything, but more willing to risk asking than to risk doing things wrong. Stan picked up a mug and indicated with his fingernail.

'About there,' he said, and then thrust the mug into her hand, grinned at her, and went up to the other end of the bar to serve a customer.

Janet managed the two drinks without too much trouble, and worked out the price while she was doing it, so she was able to ask for the money as she put the drinks down, in the way that Mary did.

'And twenty B. and H.,' Andy added, staring at her hard with half a smile on his mouth.

'Benson and Hedges?' she guessed, and Andy nodded. She went to fetch them. She didn't like serving cigarettes: because the money had to go in a separate till, you had to ask the customer the total price, while holding in your head the two other prices, of the drinks alone and of the cigarettes alone, and more often than not she forgot one or other of them, and had to start the calculation again, which made her slow, which in turn made her flustered. This time when she got back and quoted the new total, Dave said, 'Would you like· a drink yourself?' and when she had accepted she realized that all her totals would have to be worked out again. She felt all fingers and thumbs, and was miserable with the feeling of helplessness and stupidity. She put her drink down on her edge of the counter but in front of Dave, as she had seen Mary do, and went off quickly to serve someone else, as far away from Andy's witty comments as possible. When she eventually came back for her drink, she had calmed down somewhat, and since there was a let-up in the rate of customers, she was able to sip her drink and talk to Andy and Dave, and feel, for the first time, the pleasant sense of power it gave one to be on the other side of a counter for a change. If she could only learn the prices and be able to find the bottled beer she wanted first time, she thought she would enjoy this job.

Mary came back and walked straight up to Andy, who was something of a favourite with her.

'Hello, Mary, my love. How's your little protégée doing then?' Andy asked her.

'What – Janet?' Mary asked, and smiled at her encouragingly. 'She's fine. She'll be the best barmaid in Notting Hill Gate by the time she's been with us a fortnight.'

'Yes, I thought you'd be grateful to me,' Andy said, preening himself. Mary let her accent show as she said, 'It was Janet I was complimenting, not yourself.'

'It comes to the same thing,' Andy said with a proprietary smile. Janet felt a little uneasy. Andy was a clown, and made great parade of being conceited, but *was* it all in fun? She often felt that he was serious when he said these outrageous things, and supposing he was expecting more gratitude from her than she wanted to give? She felt she must tear herself away quickly, and said, 'I'll leave you to fight it out. I'm wanted.' She scuttled up to the end of the bar, and fortunately, as she got there, someone came up for service, so she had an excuse to stay there for a while. She must be a little more careful with Andy in future, just in case he was thinking of her as a girl-friend. She liked him, and was grateful for his looking after her, but she didn't want to get involved with him in any other way. She shook her head. Perhaps she was being conceited, thinking that he paid her more attention than anyone else. She must simply guard her tongue and play it by ear.

'Pint of keg, please miss,' a voice said just in front of her, and to her pleasure her hand reached spontaneously for a pint mug before she had really registered what had been said – she was on her way towards being an instinctive barmaid!

CHAPTER SEVEN

Mary's prophecy was a long way towards being fulfilled. Janet found that, once she had learnt the prices, she was able to relax, and not only did she make an efficient barmaid, but at the end of two weeks she discovered that she really enjoyed it. It was pleasant to be able to mix conversation with work, and it was pleasant to be able to chat up all the good-looking young men who came in without necessarily meaning it, for behind the bar one was safe. A barmaid's line in chat was as much a part of her job as a uniform would be, and there were few who would take it seriously and ask her out.

Janet could now serve very quickly, which was necessary, as they were busy most nights. She could serve two people at once and not mix up the prices; she had learnt how to pour two light ales into glasses at the same time; she could make a Black Velvet, a port-and-lemon, or a snowball; she could uncap a bottle at the same time as pouring a pint, and still keep an eye on the sink which she had left filling. She could wash up three or four glasses at once and dry them in the time it took one customer to pick up his drinks and leave the bar and another to take his place; she had learnt the differing techniques of pouring the perfect Worthington and the perfect Guinness; and she was no longer thrown into a panic by the expressions 'Dirty Dick', 'Liffey', 'Black and Tan', 'Mackie', or 'half-and-half'.

Stan had put her wages up to two pounds straight away, and she had a pewter mug up on the shelf, where she kept her tips, that filled rapidly. She was popular with the customers, well-liked by Mary, and thoroughly happy inside, for now she had a job that was varied and interesting, and one that she enjoyed. Of course, since she worked most evenings, she couldn't go out much to 'see the sights', but this had the advantage of allowing her to avoid Andy. It was a long day – about eleven and a half hours all told – and she got very tired at first, but once she had got her second wind she was able to get up at a reasonable hour in the morning, which meant she did not waste the time before she had to be in at the pub. Andy came to the pub sometimes while she was working, but unless he came during a morning session, and even then, early, she was usually too busy to do more than exchange a remark with him as she flew by.

Once or twice on her times off she had gone with him up to the studios, and she enjoyed this, and was learning a lot of the television jargon, but she hardly saw Sandra or her friends for the whole fortnight, and she was beginning to get the feeling that she was standing on her own two feet at last.

It was a Tuesday morning, and Janet was standing behind the bar just after opening time, reading a letter which had arrived for her that morning from home. In spite of Sandra's warning, or even maybe because of it, she had mentioned in her letter home that she had taken a job as a barmaid and was enjoying it, and her mother's reply was what she had expected.

'I'm glad to hear that you've a job. You don't mention what the pay is – I hope they aren't cheating you. What sort of a pub is it? I'm glad you like it there, but do be careful going home afterwards won't you?'

She laughed aloud at this, and then started, realizing that there was someone standing in front of her. She looked up quickly, and there, smiling down at her with a quizzical expression, was the dark-haired young man she had seen over by the door the first time she had come to this pub.

Janet felt the blood coming to her cheeks, and was aware of her heart thumping faster than usual, though she couldn't think why. The young man was looking directly at her with a very penetrating blue-eyed gaze.

'Don't let me disturb you,' he said. 'That was a lovely little smile you gave then.'

'I was just reading a letter from home,' Janet said by way of explanation. She felt confused, absurdly shy. 'What were you wanting?' she asked, needing to do something while she recovered her poise.

'I'll have a Worthington, please,' he said. 'And one for yourself.'

'It's a bit early for me, thanks all the same,' she said, and

72

hastened to get his drink, aware that he was still watching her closely. He continued to do so all the time she was pouring his drink and ringing up his money, and that done, she felt she had to go back and stand by him, for he was the only person in the bar – it was Mary's morning off.

'Cheers,' said the young man, and drank. 'Tell me, please don't think I'm rude,' he put his elbows on the bar and leaned forward, with an air of coming to the point, 'but do I know you? You seem to be haunting me, for you turn up in all sorts of places. First I saw you in Portobello Road, then in here with Dick Murray, then in the bar at the television centre, then in the studios apparently very thick with the production team, and now you turn up here again, but as a barmaid.' He smiled engagingly. 'And I have this strange feeling that I know you from way back. Do I? Have we met?'

'I don't know,' Janet said shyly. 'I first saw you over there by the door, and I thought you seemed familiar, but I can't think when we've ever met. I suppose we can't have really. Though I'm sure ...' a thought struck her. 'You must be the phantom swing door! *That's* why I keep getting this goosey feeling someone's looking at me!'

'What on earth is the phantom swing door?' he asked, laughing, and Janet told him.

'So you see, if you saw me in all those places,' she finished up, 'it must have been you that I just failed to see going out.'

'It could well be. Well, I'm glad I've solved your mystery for you, but how about solving mine for me? How come you turned up in all those places with all those different people?'

'Well, I share a flat with a girl who works at the television centre, and she goes out with Richard Murray, and she introduced me to a lot of her friends. I was with a group of them when I first saw you – I wasn't with Dick, as you thought, it just happened that we were standing next to each other.'

'In the same group.'

'Yes. And one of the group is a cameraman, and he invited me to the studios one time, because I said I'd be interested to see, and that about explains everything, I think.'

'Except why I feel I know you,' he said. Janet considered,

and then he added, 'If you told me your name, that might help.'

'Janet Anderson,' she said. He shook his head.

'Doesn't strike any bells.'

'What's yours?'

'Roger Jowitt,' he said, and immediately Janet realized why she had felt she recognized him. Some months before, in an episode of a regular detective series on the television, the villain had been supposed to come from Leeds, and had done a very good accent, and had impressed Janet by his acting and his looks so much that she had bothered, as one rarely does, to look out at the end of the programme for the credits, to see who had played the part. The name, which had meant nothing to her, had been Roger Jowitt, and as soon as he mentioned it, it brought it back to her. She was about to exclaim, and tell him, when she remembered Dick Murray's reaction to being 'recognized', and held her tongue. She didn't want to offend him, and on further thought it occurred to her that if she did 'recognize' him aloud, it would put a distance between them, that of actor and audience.

Hoping that he hadn't seen the light of realization dawn in her eye, she smiled politely and said, 'How do you do?' and he gave a relieved sort of smile that made her glad she had chosen not to mention the matter.

'How do you do?' he said, and extended his hand across the bar for her to shake. 'Now you must have a drink with me, to cement our friendship.' She noticed that his accent was quite unlike the Leeds talk in the television programme – he spoke like a southerner.

'All right, since it's a special occasion,' she said, 'I'll have a bottle of cider, thank you.'

She poured it and took his money, and then, glad there were no other customers in, went back to stand in front of him and enjoy a conversation. He really was remarkably good-looking – as Vicky would have said 'Too handsome to be let out alone' – with a broad, fair-skinned face, large blue eyes nicely set beneath fine brows and emphasized by high cheekbones. His nose was straight and his mouth, though thin, was wide and humorous. To finish it off, he was tall and well-built, and had

74

very dark, straight, shiny hair. Janet, looking closely at him now, noticed again what had attracted her attention when she had seen him on the television – almost on the point of the cheekbone below his left eye was a small brown 'beauty-spot', which had the effect of drawing attention to his eyes, like underlining a heading.

'Do you work up at the television centre?' Janet asked by way of opening the conversation.

'Oh, only on and off, but recently I've been up there a lot. That's why I've seen you so often. I was wondering —'

'Yes?' Janet prompted him.

'Well, I don't want to sound rude, but, I was wondering why you became a barmaid. One doesn't really expect nice girls to be barmaids, except in clubs and private bars.'

'That's what my flat-mate said. It surprises me how people still think like that in these enlightened times,' Janet said, but she smiled to show she was not annoyed. 'I never even thought about whether it was what nice girls did or not. I like meeting people and chatting to them, and I was fed up to the back teeth with working in an office, so this seemed ideal really.'

'And do you like it?'

'Oh yes, I enjoy it very much. Of course, it's hard work, and some nights I'm bushed by the time I get out, but I'm quite happy here.'

'Wouldn't you have rather got a job in a club bar – like the one at the Centre for instance? I would have thought that would be better than a public bar.'

'You're taking my welfare to heart, aren't you?' Janet smiled, and answered him, 'No, I wouldn't really. I like the club, and I like to go there now and again for a drink, but I'd hate to be there all the time.'

'Why?'

'Oh, I don't think I could stand it. All those actors parading around waiting to be recognized —' she pulled herself up short and blushed, remembering that he was an actor, and then blushed deeper, remembering that she wasn't supposed to know he was an actor. She picked up a drying cloth and looked about for a glass of dry, to cover up for her mistake, but Roger was looking closely at her, and after a moment he said, 'You

75

do know who I am, don't you?' She hesitated, and he insisted. 'Don't you?'

'Yes,' Janet admitted. 'I realized as soon as you said your name. You played that crook in that episode of "Jason" – the one who hid the drugs in the poodle's collar.'

'Fancy you remembering that!' he said with genuine surprise. 'I should think you're the only person in the country who remembers me in that. Everyone else knows me as the butcher in "Maple Street".'

'Oh, I've never watched that,' Janet said.

'Well, that explains it. But tell me, if you knew who I was when I told you my name, why did you pretend you didn't?'

Janet looked embarrassed again, but told him, 'Well, it's rather silly really. But when Sandra, that's my flat-mate, introduced me to Richard Murray, the way she said his name made me think she was proud of going out with somebody famous, and I thought it would disappoint her if I didn't say something about it. So I said to him, I've seen you on the telly as Dr. Booth, and he gave me such a look! If looks could kill, I'd have shrivelled up on the spot.'

'I see, so you thought that all television actors hated being recognized, and you were just being polite, in pretending you'd never seen me before.'

'Yes, exactly,' Janet said, and Roger burst into laughter. 'Well, it's all very well you laughing, but how is one to know? These stars are so touchy.'

'I wouldn't call Dick Murray a star, and me even less,' Roger said, still laughing. 'I'm not making fun of you – please don't think that. I think you're marvellously polite and thoughtful, not wanting to offend people. But it is funny —' and he was off in another gale of laughter. Janet smiled a little, but her smile quickly faded as her annoyance rose.

'Now look here,' she said eventually. 'I don't mind being laughed at, but I don't like being patronized, which is exactly what you're doing now by playing to the gallery like that. It wasn't all that funny, so stop laughing.'

That stopped him short, and he looked at her with slight embarrassment, and some guilt.

'You're right,' he said after a moment. 'Thank you for telling me.'

'Look, I didn't mean to offend you,' Janet began, feeling rather awful.

'No, I'm glad you did say that,' Roger interrupted. 'You see, when you act for a living, you not only have to do it on stage, but you have to do a lot of acting of roles to impress casting directors and so on, and apart from that, moving in acting circles tends to make you a bit theatrical. I always despise actors who put on airs, but it's fatally easy to slip into it without knowing. I really am grateful to you for pointing it out.'

'I could have been a bit more polite about it,' Janet said, still feeling apologetic.

'You could have,' he agreed, smiling, 'but then why the hell should you? If someone's making a prize ass of himself, there's no reason to spare his feelings. I don't count it a particular virtue to suffer fools gladly.'

'I never have been able to do that,' Janet said, 'patience not being one of my virtues.'

'One you don't need, having so many others,' he said lightly.

'Steady,' Janet warned. 'You're at it again.'

'No, I meant it that time,' Roger protested, 'though it's nice that you're keeping my interests at heart. Look, can I thank you by taking you out to dinner tonight?'

'I'm working,' Janet said regretfully.

'Well, so am I, of course – I meant after work.'

'I don't finish until about half past eleven,' she warned.

'That's all right – I never feel it's civilized to eat dinner earlier than ten-thirty anyway.' There was the hint of a patronizing manner slipping through there, Janet thought, but she let it by this once, though if he was going to be the Sophisticated Big City Guy showing the country cousin how to live, she would soon jump on his head. 'Can I pick you up here?' he went on.

'Yes, all right, that would be lovely,' Janet said. 'I'll try and get finished a bit earlier. Come in at five to eleven and you can wait in here for me while I clear up.'

'No, best not, in case it gets you into trouble. I'll wait outside in my car.'

'As long as you don't get pinched for loitering.'

'If anyone asks I'll say I'm filming, hidden camera in an upstairs room across the street – that sort of thing.'

'My God, it does get in the blood, doesn't it?'

'I'm fooling,' he assured her solemnly. 'Where would you like to go for dinner?'

'I wouldn't know anywhere, I'm new to the city. Make it somewhere in the West End if you can, so I can write home and tell them I've been there.'

'All right, the West End it shall be, though I've a strong feeling you're taking the mickey out of me.'

Janet raised her eyebrows. 'Now would I do a thing like that?'

She left a note at home for Sandra – 'Will be back very late – going out for dinner. Don't put the chain on. Love, J.' – and took a change of clothes with her to the pub. It wasn't really the ideal arrangement, she thought grimly, being picked up here, for after a heavy evening she really needed a bath before she was approachable; the smell of cigarettes hung about her, and her hands were as steeped in the smell of stale beer as the wood of a vinegar barrel with vinegar. She took along her tin of deodorant, and a nail brush, and hoped she would have time for a quick scrub and spray before leaving.

Mary was in the bar when she arrived, and looked askance at the carrier bag Janet carried.

'Hello, love. What've you got there?'

'Change of clothes,' Janet said, stooping to thrust her handbag down behind the Shandy bottles in the bottom bin. 'I've got a date tonight, after closing time.'

'Andy?' Mary asked.

'No, a new one. You may see him, if he comes in this evening. Very handsome, glamorous type.'

'Lucky girl,' Mary said, smiling warmly. 'I'm glad for you – hope you have a nice time. It can be lonely in London if you don't find friends and settle in somewhere.'

'I seem to be settling as quick as Rennies, don't I?' Janet said with a little wonder in her voice. 'Almost as if I was made for this place.'

'It's all in the personality,' Mary said wisely. 'Some can, some can't.'

Not much more you can say after that, thought Janet. 'I'll just pop this upstairs.'

'O.K., love. You can stop a bit early if you like, tonight. I can finish up the glasses, and we can do the rest together to-morrow.'

'Thanks, Mary. I'd like to have a bit of a wash before I meet him.'

If Roger did come into the pub that evening, Janet was too busy to notice him – so busy, in fact, that she would not have been ready before half past eleven, had not Stan, after a whisper from Mary, taken the mug she was filling out of her hand and said, 'Go on, push off. It's nearly eleven, and Romeo will be getting fed up.'

'Thanks, Stan,' she said, grabbed her handbag, and shot out before anyone else could catch her eye. It was unfortunate that tonight of all nights she had sloshed beer all down her legs so that she smelled pretty much like a four-ale bar. I'll just have to wash them, she thought, and locking herself in the little lavatory she stripped off her stockings and washed her legs at the little hand-basin, which was quite a tricky piece of balanc-ing. You've missed your vocation, lass – you should be in a circus, she told herself drily. She changed the water and washed her face and hands and lower arms, scrubbing the bits that could take it with the nail brush she had brought.

Back in the rest-room she put on the clean tights, and then quickly changed her skirt and jumper for the black dress she had brought with her. It hadn't taken much thought to decide on that, for, not knowing if he was going to take her to a formal or informal place, she had had to pick the only thing she had that would do, at a pinch, for either. It was of fine black wool, very plain, with a fitted bodice, a round neck, and a square 'yoke' of white inset. At any rate, you couldn't take offence at it, she thought. She inspected her watch and face simultaneously, and for an anxious moment couldn't decide between punctuality and paint, but then decided that the dress was really so plain that it needed a little backing up, and she forced herself to apply the necessary make-up with a slow, calm hand. No use looking like a bench that's been sat on before t'paint's dry, she thought, using one of Vicky's expressions. She hoped that the evening would be memorable enough to write to Vicky about – she owed her a letter.

In the end it was only twenty-past when she ran down the back stairs and let herself out into the alley. Roger was sitting in his car at the front of the pub, smoking a cigarette and looking very relaxed – so relaxed in fact that she had to tap on the window to attract his attention.

'I'm sorry, I was miles away,' he said as he opened the door. She slid in as gracefully as she could, which wasn't all that gracefully since he only had a white Viva. They haven't built a car that women can get into gracefully since the fifties, Janet thought, and was going to remark the same to him, but she thought it might sound like a slight on his car, and didn't.

'Sorry you had to wait so long,' she said.

'That's all right. I didn't expect you any sooner,' he said. 'You look very nice.' He leaned towards her and for a moment she thought he was going to kiss her, but he only offered her a cigarette.

'Thank you,' she said shortly, covering both the compliment and the fag.

'I hope you're hungry enough for a full dinner – I've booked a table at a restaurant I know near Leicester Square.'

'I haven't eaten since about half past four, so I can probably do justice to anything you put in front of me,' Janet said agreeably. 'Leicester Square's near Piccadilly, isn't it?'

'Yes, of course,' Roger answered absently, watching for a chance to slip out on to the Bayswater Road, and then glanced at her in surprise. 'So you weren't joking about never having been to the West End before?'

'No, why should I? I've only been in London three weeks, and most of that time I've been working.'

'I would never have known,' Roger said. 'You seem so at home here. I'm impressed.'

'What by?' Janet asked, laughing.

'Your self-sufficiency. Usually you can spot a girl on her first visit to London a mile off.'

'I'm not like the ordinary girl,' Janet said.

'I can see that,' Roger answered gravely.

They didn't do any more serious talking until they were in the restaurant, for Roger had to point out to her all the places they passed, and then he had to concentrate on finding somewhere to park. The restaurant was small and dark and crowded, even though it was so late, but they had a little table to themselves over against the wall, which was nice and private but still gave a good view of the whole place. There was a candle in a bottle on the table, whose steady glow reflected off a bunch of fat golden onions hanging on the wall above the table, and there was a soothing, subdued hum of voices having intimate conversations all around. Very romantic, Janet thought, but rather wasted on anyone who isn't in love.

'D'you like it?' Roger asked, seeing her look round with interest.

'Very much. This is what I was expecting to see a lot of when I came down here.'

'You've got expensive tastes,' Roger laughed. 'Recognize anyone here?'

'Should I?'

'That depends on your interests. But I can see at least three film stars that I should think everyone has heard of.'

That kept Janet occupied until the first course was served, and she finally managed to pick out just one of the three.

'Over there,' she nodded, 'in the green dress, it looks like Sarah Dean, but I can't see who the other two you mean are.'

'The man with Sarah Dean is Michael Tynan,' Roger said, obviously amused.

'He looks different in the flesh,' Janet said. 'I wouldn't have known him. Who's the other one?'

'Behind me and to my right, with the cigarette holder, that's Tom Barry.'

Janet searched hard, and finally found the resemblance. She was quite shocked.

'He looks like an old man,' she said finally.

'That's show biz,' Roger said, laughing at her. She drew herself up stiffly.

'I don't think you ought to shatter my illusions – it isn't kind.'

'Now that's what I wouldn't expect you to have – illusions. You seem to have your head screwed firmly on the right way. How's the avocado pear, by the way?'

'Very nice,' she said politely, and thought, the hell, honesty's the best whatnot after all. 'Very dull. Not what I expected.'

'Oh dear, I can see I'm failing miserably. You'll be telling them all back home what a boring place London is and how the people there don't know how to live.'

'With a capital L?' Janet laughed at him. 'Really, we aren't that innocent in the frozen north, you know.'

'I do know – I lived in Sheffield for a while, doing Rep. But tell me, where do you come from?'

'I don't expect you've heard of it – a town called Matsley.' He shook his head. 'Where's it near?'

She thought for a moment. 'I should think the only place it's near that you'd have heard of is Leeds.' He nodded.

'And what did you do there? Tell me all about you. Do you want something else instead of that avocado, by the way?'

'No, I'll eat it now I've got it. It's quite nice really.' He was leaning forward, waiting for her to begin, and she gave a little smile. 'Don't look so eager – there isn't anything to tell about me – I've never done anything interesting.'

'Tell me anyway. It'll be interesting to me.'

Now that was a nice encouraging remark, she thought, one to be stored up and pondered over. 'Well,' she began, 'I was born in Matsley at a very early age, of parents. I went to the local school, then went to secretarial college, then went to work for a local firm. Went out in the evenings sometimes, found life very boring. And that's all.'

'Why did you decide to come down here? I mean, how did it happen?'

'Well, I've this friend called Vicky, and she used to write to Sandra, who was in the same class with her, and Sandra wrote one time to say her flat-mate was leaving, and Vicky said why didn't I share with her, and here I am.'

'That's very adventurous of you, just to up and leave like that. I don't think I'd have had the nerve,' Roger said, with the air of one who wants to be asked the appropriate question.

Obediently Janet said, 'What about you then? Tell me your history.' I sound like the Griffon, she thought.

'Well, I come from High Wycombe originally,' Roger began, and, wickedly, Janet interrupted.

'You do a very good Yorkshire accent for a southerner.'

'Sorry?' He looked vague.

'When you were in "Jason". That's why I first noticed you. I thought it was natural.'

'I've always been quite good at accents, and impersonations in general. That's why I decided to try acting as a career. My family were against it, except Mum.'

'Why?' Janet asked promptly.

'Well, they thought it was a chancey sort of thing to get mixed up in, no security you know. Then Dad started his own business and did pretty well out of it, and Mum began to get ideas above her station – and the acting fitted in with that. She saw me taking her to first-nights and press receptions and so on. Of course, she pretty soon found out it wasn't like that, but by then the riches bug had worn off, so it didn't really matter.'

'Do they still live in – wherever it is?'

'High Wycombe. Yes, in the same old house. I go and see them quite often. I'd like to take you one time – you'd like them, I should think. Dad can be really funny when he tries.'

Janet was glad that the waiter arrived at that moment, saving her from having to answer, for being invited to a boy's home was, in her part of the world, a very serious thing, and she was not sure if the custom were different here, or if Roger was far more serious about her than he had any right to be on their first evening out.

'So,' she said at last, making conversation. 'You're just a nice ordinary boy from a nice ordinary home, and you want me around to take you down a peg now and again, so as to keep you unspoilt for the girl-next-door, who's waiting back home for you to make your fortune, and then snatch her up on to the back of your white horse and ride away with her into the sunset. Slow fade. The End. Lights come up and Janet syruptitiously dabs her eyes with a hanky.'

Roger gazed at her admiringly. 'My, but you've a nasty sharp tongue when you've a mind, lass,' he said in a parody of a Yorkshire accent. Janet laughed.

'You've not 'eard the 'alf of it, my lad,' she countered. 'I'm goin' to keep you firmly in control from now on.'

'All for the benefit of the girl-next-door?'

'Now there's a silly question,' Janet answered, leaving him to draw his own inferences from that. I'm turning out to be quite good at this repartee business, she thought.

CHAPTER EIGHT

'Dear Vicky,

I feel rather guilty about not writing to you all this time, except that one short letter, so I'm making up for it now with All the News. The excuse is as usual – I've been so busy. You don't realize until you do it how much time being a barmaid takes up. I have to be in at half past ten at the latest to get ready for morning opening, and what with clearing up and chucking people out, I don't finish until at least half past three. Then I have to be back on at five to get ready for the evening session, and don't usually finish that until eleven-thirty, so you can see there isn't much time to spare. I'm actually writing this in my supper-hour in the rest-room upstairs, so if you can hear sounds of revelry it's probably Big Paddy singing in the bar downstairs. He's got a nice voice really, it's a pity singing isn't allowed. He'll probably be banned again for a week.

Well, in answer to your most important query, the answer at the time you asked was No. There was a sort of friend of Sandra's called Andy who I think had taken a shine to me, but it was purely one-sided, and after I came to work here, he took the hint and shied off, and we're just friendly. I wouldn't want not to be friendly with him as he gets me in to the B.B.C. place when I've nothing else to do.

But back to business – you'll be glad to know that the answer is now Yes, and he's actually someone you'll probably know, being a telly fiend! His name's Roger Jowitt, and he plays the butcher in "Maple Street", which I can proudly admit to never seeing in my life. I think Roger's rather glad about that, as he seems to think playing in 'Maple Street' is something to be ashamed of rather than otherwise, so if you ever meet him don't come blurting out with it, or he'll probably give me up.

Anyway, he's very nice – of course, you'll know what he looks like, or if you don't, watch the telly on Thursday night at eight o'clock, and you will, so I don't need to go into raptures about his blue eyes etc. He seems to like me very much and I must say I'm fetched with him, though he has a funny way of slipping into these sort of theatrical attitudes when he forgets himself. I don't care much for that sort of conceit, and tell him as much pretty sharply, but he takes it in good part, which is a hopeful sign that he may not be too far gone to save!

You ask how I get on with Sandra – well, to tell you the truth, I don't – we hardly ever see each other. She works odd hours, though mostly office sort of hours, and I work odd hours and nearly every evening, so it hardly ever happens that we're in the house at the same time. It's probably a good thing, as I get very annoyed at the state she leaves the kitchen in. Sometimes I feel like leaving it like that as a protest, but then I realize it'd be me that I'd be punishing, not her, as she obviously doesn't care what state it's in. Still, as I hardly ever see her I can't have rows with her over it. In any case, it's me sharing her flat, not vice versa, so I don't really feel entitled to mention it. Probably I'm wrong in that – Roger says I am – but you know me, always thinking about other people's feelings (Ha ha).

It's turned very hot this past week – trying to make up for the rotten summer I suppose, so I hope you're getting a bit of this sunshine and blue sky. I have a day off tomorrow, which fortunately falls at the same time as one of Roger's, so we're going out for the day. We're taking a boat trip down the river to Windsor, where the Queen lives (it says here), and we'll find a nice quiet field, full of daisies and shady trees, and – dot dot dot. You don't think I'm going to tell you all my secrets do you? Some hopes!

Why don't you come down for a weekend? If you can get off work early on Friday you could be down here before closing time, and then you could meet my Beloved. Actually, I am getting quite fond of him, heaven help me. I don't suppose Sandra would mind you staying over the weekend, especially since you're her friend, more than I was. Has she written to you, by the way? She came over all motherly when I first told her about Roger, and warned me about the Evil Ways of actors, which is quite something considering she goes out with

Richard Murray (yes, *The* Richard Murray, fans, no less!). She said not to get too attached to Rodge as he would Break My Heart (she really did use those words) and, to do her justice, she did seem genuinely concerned, though I can't think why, Roger not being the type who could hurt a flea.

I must stop now – time to get back to work, hey ho! The post office will probably refuse to take this letter on account of the cruelty to animals act not letting the pony express take more than three tons weight. In any case, I shall never get it into an envelope. So if you get it, it will be because Someone up there likes you, not the G.P.O.

God bless!
Janet.'

Janet put down the ballpoint and flexed her aching fingers. The heat of her hand had made the ink run, and her right hand was pale blue. She felt disagreeably damp, despite wearing nothing but bra and knicks, a cotton skirt, and a sleeveless, low-cut cotton blouse – but it really was hot in here, almost airless. It was time for her to be back downstairs, so she folded the letter and thrust it into the envelope she had already addressed, and after squashing it and pressing it hard managed to seal the flap. She dashed into the lavatory and washed her hands, and then made her way downstairs.

The bar doors were open, and a lot of people were outside on the pavement in the evening sun, which gave the place an agreeably continental air, but the day was so humid and airless that no breeze came in through the open doors to relieve the sweltering staff. Mary looked moist and limp, but still indefatigably cheerful, while Stan was a boiled red colour that made Janet fear for his blood-pressure.

Roger had arrived while she was upstairs, and was leaning against the bar opposite one of the doors with a cold light ale, and with him, to Janet's surprise, were Dick Murray and Sandra.

'Ey-oop!' Dick said facetiously, by way of greeting, and Janet gave him a withering sort of smile.

'Hello you two, what're you doing out in the wilds of Notting Hill? Hello, Roger,' the last with a little more warmth, and receiving a special smile that made her heart thump for a moment.

'Oh we just thought we'd drop in and see you at work, since we were passing this way,' Sandra said. Her accent, Janet noticed, became more aggressively southern when she was with Dick – no slips into dialect, the way she sometimes did at home with just Janet to hear her.

'Actually, they were about to go in the "Hoop" when I saw them,' Roger said. 'I was shocked at such treachery, but I forgave them once they'd bought me a drink.'

'Talking of which, would you like something?' Richard asked Janet.

'Well, thanks, I will – I'll just have a cold lemonade. I have to keep drinking to keep cool, so I have to lay off the beer or I'd be too spiffy to pour straight.'

She went down to the cold bins and got her lemonade, and rang up the money, and when she rejoined the group, Richard said, 'I never noticed before that you go barefoot. Isn't it rather dangerous?'

'Not really,' Janet answered, used to being asked this. 'Mary and I never break glasses, though of course I wouldn't go round your side without shoes.'

'But why on earth do you do it?' he wanted to know.

'Well, it's too hot to wear stockings, and my shoes rub my heels if I wear them without,' Janet said. Roger grinned wickedly.

'That's not the real reason! Tell him the truth, Janet.'

'He'll think I'm nutty.'

'Of course he will. What does it matter?'

'Do tell – it all sounds very mysterious,' Richard said, Sandra looked aloof, knowing the answer.

'It isn't at all, really, it's just common sense,' Janet said. 'When you're on your feet all day in this weather, they get very hot and swollen. There's always a lot of beer spilt behind the bar, and paddling in it keeps my feet cool. That's all.'

Richard roared with laughter.

'I think that's priceless. Sort of wine-treading in reverse.'

'Ah, there's lots of little tricks to keeping cool,' Janet said. 'You see Mary there? You notice she always stands in the same position, with her hands behind her?'

'Yes, what of it?'

'She has this theory that whatever temperature your wrists are, the rest of you stays that temperature. Well, where she's standing are the cold bins – the refrigerated shelves – and she sticks her hands in them to keep them cold.'

'What a clever idea,' Roger said. 'You never told me that one before.'

'Oh, that's nothing,' Janet said airily. 'The barmaid in the "Devonshire" keeps a handkerchief full of ice cubes in one of the ice buckets, and when no-one's looking she sticks it under her arm-pits.'

'I don't suppose the customers who want ice in their whisky like it much,' Sandra said.

'All right if you like it salty,' Dick said quickly, and Roger laughed.

'You could always dip your crisps in.'

'I was just writing to Vicky, in my break,' Janet said to Sandra. 'Have you written to her at all?'

'Not recently – why?'

'I just wondered if I was duplicating news, that's all.'

'No – I don't often write. Never was much good with a pen.' She looked meaningfully at Dick, but whatever it was he was supposed to say, he missed his cue.

'Anybody for another?' Roger asked, and Sandra broke in quickly, 'Oh, no, we'll have to be getting along. We only just dropped in for one, to see Janet. We can't stay.'

Dick opened his mouth and shut it again, and Roger just smiled, not attempting to change her mind, and in a moment they had gone. Janet went off to serve someone, and when she came back, and opened another bottle for Roger without his needing to ask, she said, 'What's bitten her? Did we offend her?'

'You should know what's wrong,' Roger said. 'It's obvious.'

'What's obvious? I don't know what you mean.'

'Well, didn't you see the way old Dick was looking at you?'

'No,' Janet said, genuinely surprised, then, 'You're imagining things. I didn't see anything special in the way he looked.'

'My dear girl, you're too modest. Naturally poor Sandra's

jealous. There you are, stunningly attractive, full of lively conversation, looking so efficient behind the bar. No wonder Dick couldn't take his eyes off you. I was on the verge of dotting him one myself.'

Janet blushed, and tried to laugh it off.

'I don't know where you think flattery's going to get you,' she began, but Roger cut her short.

'I'm not flattering. I mean every word,' he said seriously. 'And tomorrow, when I get you alone and we have time to talk, I'm going to tell you a lot of things about you, so you'd better get used to the idea.'

Janet hardly dared look at him, and felt sure he could see her heart hammering. What could he mean? She thought she knew, and yet that seemed a lot to assume, when they had only known each other such a short time. She took the courage to look up, and his bright blue eyes were gazing into hers with an expression that made her feel quite weak. Then he smiled.

'You'd better go and serve that man down there, or we'll be arrested for indecent behaviour in public.'

That was more like it, Janet thought as she moved down the bar to serve. Now was not the time for getting serious; but she was looking forward to tomorrow with a mixture of excitement and trepidation.

The Sunday was as fine a day as its predecessors had been, and in the quiet of the morning they set off, taking the tube to Charing Cross pier to get the boat. Roger looked terrific, Janet thought, in very dark blue velvet trousers, pink shirt, and a jacket which he carried over his arm – every bit the film-star, especially with that terrific tan he had gained over the past lovely week. Janet was wearing a very plain, sleeveless linen dress, white with a sprigged pattern in lilac on it, and her hair was loose, held back by a white hair-band. Roger didn't often comment on the way she looked or dressed, but today, as they filed slowly on board the boat, he smiled at her against the sun and said, 'You look really lovely. That style suits you – you don't need elaborate clothes or hair-dos.'

Janet smiled back, for once at a loss for words, and then said, to keep the tone light, 'Will you let me do everything I want today? Even have a cream tea? I've always wanted one of those, but when we were little my mum said they weren't worth the money, and when we were a bit older my sister said they were too touristy.'

'You can have anything you ask for today,' Roger said. 'I couldn't refuse you anything.'

They didn't talk much on the trip down river. Fortunately there was no running commentary on this trip, so they could just sit quietly and enjoy the scenery. They sat up in the bows, and the sun danced dazzlingly on the water, and a little soft breeze moved their hair and made a little relief from the heat.

'This will give you a tan,' Roger said. 'You're pale with all that working indoors.'

Windsor was already crowded when they arrived, and after seeing the multitudes filing into the castle, Janet said she would take the inside on trust.

'I can buy some postcards to send home – they'll never know I didn't really "do" it properly.'

'All right,' Roger said indulgently. 'It might be an idea to have lunch now, before everyone else gets the same idea. It might be difficult to get a place later on.'

They found a place – a hotel in the town – and Janet said 'I've always wanted to eat lunch at a hotel. It seems a very posh thing to do.'

'Posher than having dinner in a restaurant in Leicester Square?' Roger asked her, amused. She considered.

'I think so. It's a different kind of posh. The restaurant was just having a lot of money, but a hotel is sort of upper-class posh.'

'I know what you mean,' Roger said sympathetically.

'I should hope you do,' Janet said sharply. 'You shouldn't be hardened and cynical at your age.'

The dining room of the hotel was cool and dark, with lots of dark panelling, windsor chairs (appropriately enough) with chintz-covered cushions tied on their seats, and a large black cat that dozed on the window seat. It opened one eye as they came in and added its purring to the slow ticking of the grand-father clock, which was the only other sound in the peaceful room, for it was early for lunch and they were the first in.

They chose iced melon and roast-beef salad, and then Roger

said he'd have apple pie and cream, while Janet wanted fresh strawberries. Roger chose a wine to go with it all, and they ate slowly and appreciatively. Then coffee was served, and they sipped in silence, each now feeling a kind of tension building up. At last, Roger put down his cup and reached across the small table to take Janet's hand, that was fiddling with her table-mat. She looked up, not really surprised, but almost breathless with anticipation.

'What?' she said softly. Roger smiled at her, and slowly she smiled back.

'I think I'm in love with you,' he said.

'Only think?' Janet asked, feeling herself blushing again.

'No. I know I am really. Do you mind?'

'Of course I don't. How could I?' Janet said, and pressed his fingers in hers. He gave a little sigh that sounded like relief, and then said,

'Let's finish up and go. We can get a punt out – I know a place ...'

The rest of the afternoon passed like a dream. They hired a wide, shallow punt, and drifted down the river in it. Sometimes Roger rowed strongly, while Janet held the tiller ropes or trailed a hand in the water in the approved style, and sometimes Janet rowed; and sometimes they drifted under the willows while Roger sat beside her on the broad seat and kissed her. The sun beat down on them, and the water danced and sparkled and made happy little gulping noises against the boat, and there was the sound of birds in the bushes, and other boaters' voices sounding hollow across the water.

They took the boat back and then walked a little, along the towpath and through fields. Janet made a daisy-chain, a thing she hadn't done since she was very small, and wore it round her neck, and they walked on, arms around each other's waists, kissing now and then in a slow, dreamy sort of way.

The sun grew heavier and more golden as it began to descend, and they went back into the town, to the station, where they found toilets, and were able to wash the stickiness of sweat and tar off their hands, and then, in accordance with his promise, Roger found a place that advertised cream teas and they went in and had one. Janet, almost defiantly, had two different types of cream cake, each piece looking like a miniature cliff, and Roger laughed at her and said again that he loved her. It was odd, she thought, the way he seemed to come out with it in the most public places. She was in a strange way relieved that he didn't seem to ask any response from her, for she was not sure of her feelings, and didn't want to have to probe into them at this time. He seemed content just to tell her, and kiss her, without asking any reassurance.

She felt almost disappointed when they boarded the boat for the homeward journey, but on an impulse, when the boat stopped at Putney, Roger grabbed her hand and pulled her down the gangplank, and they went into a pub just opposite where there was quite a crowd of young people, and later on someone started to sing folk songs. It was the perfect end to the day.

They went home by bus, sitting on the top deck and holding hands like a couple of school kids. Janet was worried that he might expect her to invite him in, and she wondered how she could refuse him without offending him, but at the front door he took her in his arms and kissed her long and lovingly, and then said,

'I'll come in tomorrow lunchtime and see you.'

'Won't you be working?' she asked in surprise.

'Nope. We've finished recording "Maple Street" – the whole of the rest of the series – and I've nothing else on hand.'

She detected through his flippancy a slight note of anxiety, and didn't know what to say, except 'Oh.'

'So you see, today was the last expensive outing I can take you on for some time, unless something turns up quite quickly. I'm sorry.'

'Don't be silly,' Janet said. 'It doesn't matter. You don't have to spend lashings of money to enjoy yourself.'

'You mean you'd still love me if I was penniless?' he said. It was the nearest he had come to asking her if she loved him, and though he made it sound like a joke, Janet was not sure it wasn't serious.

'Money wouldn't make any difference,' she said. He seemed satisfied with that, but Janet felt he had noticed that she avoided the issue. He kissed her again, and as he turned to go she said quickly, 'I'll see you tomorrow then. Don't forget.'

'Sleep well,' he said, and gave a little wave as he turned into the street.

She did, but it was a long time before she could get off to sleep for thinking about him, and trying to discover what she felt.

CHAPTER NINE

'Dear Jan,

I was going to write to you, and this was it, but then I thought, why bother when you can visit her just as easily? So I'm not writing to you, I'm coming down. I'm catching the four-forty train on Friday, so meet me at the station please, or I might run off with a sailor, and then you wouldn't get the parcel that your Mum is sending by me.

I am coming down to sort you out. It seems as though you need it. Have yer actual Roger on hand to be met, and line me up one (or two) of his friends. I don't mind which ones, as long as they're handsome and rich and famous – I'm not fussy. The Penguin's flapping this way, and I must get this letter down to the post room before they stop, or I'll have to buy a stamp for it, and I don't love anyone that much, not even you.

See ya!

Victoria R.'

Janet laughed as she read the letter. How typical of Vicky, to send the letter so late that it only arrived on Friday morning, and to leave her, Janet, to find out when and where the train she was to meet got in. It would be nice to see her again, though. Despite settling in so well in London, Janet got a bit homesick now and again, and also felt the need of a female friend, and the only real friend she had made since she had been in London was Roger.

He was leaning against the bar at this moment, sipping his way slowly through a light ale. Poor times, she thought, watching him through her eyelashes, when a man has to make one light ale last. You could find out a lot about a person, she had discovered, by what and how he drinks. She had a sudden picture of herself in years ahead as the typical barmaid, stout and deep bosomed, leaning on the counter and dispensing good advice with the Guinnesses and homely philosophy with the halves o' Special.

95

'From my best friend at home – she's coming down for the weekend, and wants me to meet her,' Janet said to Roger, aware that he was watching her, waiting for a comment.

'When?'

'Tonight. She says she's getting the four-forty train, so I'll have to find out where that comes in, and when. I'll have to ask for time off, too. I hope Stan won't mind.'

'I shouldn't think he would,' Roger said. 'He seems to like you – I almost get jealous sometimes.'

'Don't be silly,' Janet said briskly. 'What are you doing tonight?'

'I hadn't made any plans. Why?'

'I wondered if you'd come with me to meet her, and entertain her until closing time.'

'What's she like?' Roger asked cautiously. Janet laughed.

'Oh, don't worry, she isn't a bore. She's great fun, and she's determined to meet you anyway.'

'How does she know about me? What have you been saying?'

'I've been bragging about you, of course. That's what I came to London for, to meet all these glamorous film stars and playboys.'

'Don't be silly.'

'That's my line.' They smiled at each other, and then Roger said, 'All right, I'm game. I'll look after her and make her feel at home, on one condition.'

'Ah, blackmail is it?'

'Certainly. I'm not giving up a chance to get you in my power.'

'All right, what's the condition?'

'That you don't desert me for her this weekend. Make it a threesome, eh?'

'My dear fella, I would have anyway.'

That much was true, anyhow. Roger had been in every day that week, and she had grown used to having him around. He had visited her flat at last, and on three days already that week they had gone back to the flat for lunch between sessions. It had been pleasantly domesticated, him sitting at the kitchen table buttering bread while she stood over the stove frying eggs, and when they had sat opposite each other to eat, she had even gone so far as to wonder what it would be like to breakfast with him. It seemed odd to her that she should think about marriage, without ever having felt that she was in love with him.

He was gorgeous-looking, of course, and great fun to be with, and she would have been miserable if he had left her, and she got all the right sort of exciting sensations when he kissed her, which was often, but was that the same as being in love? Vicky was right, she did need sorting out, though she doubted if Vicky really knew in what way.

'What are you thinking about?' Roger asked her curiously, and she came to with a start, realizing that she had been staring at him for several minutes.

'You,' she said.

'Well I'm glad to hear it,' Roger said with a grin. 'Oh, here's Stan, you can ask him now about that time off.'

Stan made no difficulties about the time off, and it was arranged that Janet should take the whole evening off, and come in on Sunday evening instead, swapping time off with his wife.

'It'll suit her nicely,' he said. 'She wanted to go and see her mother on Sunday, and this'll mean she won't have to hurry back.'

'I'm glad it turned out that way,' Janet said to Roger as they made their way to Euston that evening. 'I would have felt a bit guilty otherwise.'

'You are funny,' Roger said. 'Most people are only too glad to get a bit of time off, but you feel guilty.'

'Well, Stan's always so good to me,' she began to justify herself, but he took her hand and pressed it.

'I know. You're a nice girl.'

Janet felt herself blushing, and they sat in silence for a while, still holding hands. She stared at the adverts, remembering her first tube-train journey, and how odd it had seemed to her, and how she had read every word on every advert. Now she scarcely saw them, though she looked at them. She wondered if the advertisers knew what little effect their adverts had on people. If she ever wanted to go to an agency for a job, she would never go to one of those that advertised in the tube; she would pick some obscure little homely-looking one on a street corner, because it would remind her of her home town.

Roger was also looking at the adverts. The one opposite him was about some scent or other.

'Big cool tissues, drenched in – sweat,' he murmured, and she giggled.

'It seems funny to remember only a few weeks ago all this was new to me,' Janet said, reverting to her former train of thought.

'And now – does it seem like home?' Roger asked.

'In some ways I feel as if I've lived here for years, but I wouldn't like to settle here for good.'

'Why not?'

'There's something sort of false about it all. I can't quite explain it. Sort of insincere. Even the people seem to shut themselves off from you in a funny sort of way.'

'Even me?' he asked seriously.

'Oh you – you're just an ordinary old person from the provinces, like me. Nice ordinary homeloving people, not Londoners at all.'

'So that's how you see me.'

'I should hope so,' Janet said. 'Isn't that what you wanted me for in the first place, to keep your feet on the ground, to stop fame turning your head?' Roger laughed and nodded. 'So you must keep no secrets from me. Where were you this afternoon? You sounded very mysterious when you said you couldn't see me till later on.'

'Ah, now that is a secret. I want it to be a surprise for you, so don't ask me, there's a good girl,' he pleaded.

'You see, it's started already, the beginning of the end,' Janet said, and before he could find out whether she was serious or joking, she jumped up and said, 'Come on, this is our stop, and unless her train's late, poor old Vicky will be waiting up there, thinking she's been deserted.'

The train was late, and when it finally arrived Janet and Roger were standing at the barrier, and scrutinized everyone that got off. When the flood of people passing through the gates had slowed to a trickle they finally spotted Vicky walking down from the end of the train with two soldiers, one on either side of her, carrying her bags. Janet laughed aloud.

'That's her all right,' she said to Roger, 'the girl with the two squaddies. She never manages to sit still for five minutes without making a pick-up. She's an incredible girl!'

'I think I'm going to like her,' Roger said laughing, watching Vicky chatter her way towards them. She came through the barrier and dismissed her attendants.

'Well these are my friends, so I can manage from here. Thanks ever so much for the drinks and that, and don't forget to look us up if you're ever up that way. Ta-ra, well.' The two young soldiers wandered off looking rather crestfallen, and Vicky turned to them with an impish grin. 'I bet you didn't expect me to turn up with a full guard!'

'Oh Vicky, you are incredible,' Janet said.

'Well, it's a long journey, and why should I waste my well-earned money on drinks when there's fellas just itching to buy for me. Anyway, how are you, Jan? And this is the handsome and famous Roger you keep bragging about.' She screwed up her face and looked him up and down with exaggerated scrutiny. 'Yes, I think he'll pass. How d'you do?'

Roger shook hands with her and said, 'Let's go and have a drink, or are you too full already?'

'Don't ask daft questions, lad. Just lead on. I must say you two looked a pretty couple standing by the barrier there.'

'A pretty couple of what?' Roger asked.

'Don't tempt me.'

'Do you know, I've missed you, Vicky,' Janet said.

'I should think so. But you know, this man is definitely wrong for you. He's much more my type, so if you'll excuse me —' she tucked her arm into Roger's and increased her pace a little. 'He's got my type of humour. Mind you, Janet's a friend of mine, and to do her justice, she's always had good taste.' Roger's other arm was involved with holding Vicky's case, so Janet, with a small smile to herself, was forced merely to tag along on Vicky's other side.

'So tell me all the news,' Janet said when they were settled, a short time later, round a table with drinks in front of them. 'How's Emersons' getting on without me?'

'Your department isn't doing too well,' Vicky said promptly. 'They never got anyone to take over your old job, so Mrs. Landon had to do her own invoices, and it's getting her that ratty, you can hardly go near her.'

'I can't imagine her being ratty,' Janet said with surprise.

'Well, there are those who say it's got another reason,' Vicky said, with an air of settling herself down for a bit of scandal.

'And what's that?'

'She's been going out with Tom Waldron, and she's found out that he's two-timing her.'

'Who told you that?' Janet asked, astonished.

'I had it off Vera Bastowe, and she had it off Pauline – you know, his secretary.'

'And do you believe it?'

'I wouldn't believe anything Vera Bastowe said about Tom Waldron, but I'll tell you something. Pauline's the one he's supposed to have two-timed Mrs. L. with, and the week after Vera told me about it, Pauline handed in her notice, and Horace from the post room said he took a note down to Pauline from the internal, and she tore it up without even reading it, and threw it in the bin. And whose writing was that note in?'

'Not Mrs. L.'s?'

'The same.' Vicky nodded her bouffant head impressively. They were interrupted at that moment by a burst of laughter from Roger.

'Honestly, you girls!' he said.

'Don't come the high and mighty with me, my lad,' Vicky said sternly to him. 'I've heard fellas gossiping, and they're worse than us. At least we keep it clean.'

'Yes, I know, but it's still very funny,' Roger said, and Vicky smiled at him indulgently.

'All right, let's have a nice spicy bit of television gossip. Who's given a nice big leading part to whose mistress? Who scratched whose eyes out in the dressing room?'

'I wouldn't know the latest bits,' Roger said with a slightly bitter tone. 'I haven't been around the studios for ages.'

'Oh, I see – you're resting between parts, are you? Never mind, things'll change soon. I see a big breakthrough for you. Let me look at your tea-leaves. Ah yes, this swan in your teacup means you will be sailing into more fortunate waters – either that or you're sitting too near the bank and it's after your sarnie. Get out, you brute!' She made a pantomime of dragging the thing out by its neck and beating it off. 'Aunty Vicky knows all, with a capital N.A.'

'Do you read hands as well?' Roger asked her.

'No, but I've seen the film. Seriously, though, what about the news down here? No births, deaths or marriages? Especially marriages?'

'I think Sandra's pretty thick with Richard Murray,' Janet said quickly, afraid Vicky would jump in with both big feet and ask Roger an embarrassing question.

'That won't last,' Vicky said confidently. 'I've read about Richard Murray in *Reveille* – Sandra won't hold him. He likes novelty. She'd have to grow another leg or something. But what about you two?'

'What about that parcel you said you were bringing from me mam?' Janet cut across firmly, seeing the wicked twinkle in Vicky's eye.

Because Janet had to work, Vicky and Roger were together quite a lot, and they seemed to get on very well. While Janet was working on Saturday morning, Roger took Vicky to see some of the sights, Trafalgar Square and Big Ben and Horseguards Parade, and then when Janet finished they all met and had a meal, and then they took Vicky to see Piccadilly Circus, and saw a film that Vicky fancied that wasn't likely to come on general release for a long time, if at all. Then they went back to the flat and had coffee and talked, and Sandra arrived back with Dick Murray, so Vicky had her wish of meeting both the famous boy-friends. Janet had rather expected Sandra to put on airs in front of Vicky, as she had in front of Janet at first, but she seemed, on the contrary, rather subdued, as if she was scared of Vicky's tongue. Janet was forced to notice that it was Vicky who held the party together, and had to admit that her own line in repartee, of which she was rather proud, was nothing to Vicky's.

On Sunday they got up late, and Janet had to hurry to get into the pub on time. Vicky came down later after a leisurely breakfast, and sat on a stool at the corner of the bar watching

Janet work and chatting lazily. But when, at half past one, Roger turned up, she left the bar and went and sat with Roger at a table on the other side of the room, and the two of them were soon deep in conversation. Janet felt slightly annoyed, and after a prolonged probing of herself came up with the surprising result that she was jealous. She was ashamed of herself. Vicky was her best friend. Still, she was glad when the session finished and she was able to join them in the sunshine on the street and walk slowly home.

There was just time to see Vicky off before dashing back for the evening session, and though she desperately wanted to ask what the tête-à-tête had been about, she couldn't quite bring herself to do it. Roger kissed Vicky goodbye in the easy way that television people have, and then Vicky turned to Janet, and after hesitating a moment, leaned forward as if to kiss her too. This was something Vicky had never done before, and Janet was surprised, but she understood a moment later when Vicky whispered in her ear, 'He's for you, Jan. He's the best. Don't worry.' Then she added aloud, 'Ta-ra, well. I'll tell yer ma you'll be up soon.'

'Yes, I'll come for a weekend as soon as I can get the time off. Bye, Vicky.'

'Safe journey,' Roger said.

They watched her jump on the train, and then turned away and began walking back towards the underground entrance.

'Nice girl,' Roger said at last.

'I'm glad you like her,' Janet said. 'I have to go straight back to work now.'

'Shall I see you later?' Roger asked. 'You finish early tonight, don't you?'

'Yes, at ten.'

'We could go and have a hamburger or something,' he suggested. Janet smiled.

'O.K., that'd be lovely.'

Vicky hadn't said a word to Janet about the subject, but somehow, something was sorted out by the visit. She did love Roger after all, and a feeling of warmth and peacefulness came over her when he took her hand a minute later and drew it through his arm. Everything was all right.

CHAPTER TEN

About two weeks later, on a Wednesday, just after morning opening, Janet was wiping up a few glasses and listening to the rain pelting down outside, and waiting for her first customer to come in, when the bar door opened and Roger dashed in looking very excited.

'Roger! You're soaked – why on earth did you come out without a coat?' Janet exclaimed. His jumper steamed like a wet spaniel, his black hair hung over his face and dripped water down his nose and into his mouth.

'Jan, terrific news! We're celebrating! Pour two brandies, damn the expense.'

'What is it?' Janet asked, laughing at his excitement. 'You look as though you'd won the pools.'

He reached over the bar and caught her hands, and pulled her across to him and kissed her.

'My good girl, the news I've just had beats the pools hollow.'

'Well, tell me then,' she said.

'Let's have those brandies first,' he said. 'D'you want me to catch my death?'

'You can have a brandy – I can't stand the stuff,' Janet said, pouring one quickly and pushing it over the bar to him.

'Well, you must have something special, something you really like. A special toast,' Roger insisted.

'All right, I'll have a sherry, if you insist.' She poured a sherry for herself and took the pound note he tossed on to the bar and rang up the money. 'Now for goodness' sake, tell me what all the shouting's about. What's happened?'

Roger lifted his glass solemnly. 'To my new career,' he toasted, and drank.

'I'll drink to that,' Janet said, 'but what is it?'

'I won't tease you any more, poor girl,' he said, grinning

happily. 'You remember that Friday your friend came –
Vicky?'

'Yes?'

'You remember that afternoon I wasn't with you, and I said
it was a secret where I'd been?'

'Vaguely,' Janet admitted.

'Vaguely! What a girl! Well, that afternoon, I was at an
audition, and this morning, I got a letter to say I'd got the
part.' He grinned at her irrepressibly.

'Terrific!' Janet said, genuinely pleased. 'What's the part?
Something big?'

'The Beeb is doing *Pride and Prejudice* as a five-part serial,
and I'm going to play Darcy.'

'Is that good?' Janet asked.

'Haven't you ever read it? Darcy's the lead, you ignor-
amus.'

'Well, that's really good. I'm terribly pleased for you,
Rodge,' Janet said, passing by the insult.

'But the really best part about it is, this serial's going to be
very much talked about, and the lead part's going to attract a
lot of attention – it could lead to a lot of other parts, big parts.
This could be the start of something really important for me,'
Roger said. Janet had never seen him look so happy, and it was
odd that she should feel slightly uneasy. Why on earth?

'Well, I think that's marvellous,' Janet said, beginning to
run out of adjectives. 'Tell me about this serial, when do you
start?'

'We begin the rehearsals on Friday. I'll be kept pretty busy
by it, so I won't be able to see you so often of course. But since
I've only been seeing you so much because I've been out of
work, I expect you'll be glad.'

There were too many ambiguities in that for her to sort out
all at once, so she said instead of answering, 'Who's playing
the female lead? I presume there is one?'

'Certainly there is, a very important one. You really must
read the book, or you'll never know what I'm talking about.
Get it out of the library.'

'All right, bully. But who is?'

'Who is what?'

104

'Playing the female lead, you dummy!'

'Sorry – Stephanie Sayers is playing Elizabeth.'

'Stephanie Sayers! I've heard of her. I think I saw her in a late-night play once – isn't she the very good-looking tall girl? Blonde?'

'She isn't blonde, she has sort of fair-mouse hair.'

'Well it was only a black-and-white telly I saw her on,' Janet said. 'Is she the one anyway?'

'I should think so. She is tall and very good-looking. Really stunning, in fact. She's one of those women who look better with their make-up off than on.'

'A rare type,' Janet commented drily, but he didn't seem to notice. 'Hadn't you better go and get dried off?'

'Yes, I suppose so. Look, what are you doing afterwards?'

'I was going to ask you that.'

'Well, can you come over to my place, and I'll have something ready for you – to eat I mean – and then you could help me read through my script?'

'O.K., then, if you like. I'll be a bit late, because Mary wants to get off early. Will you be alone?' He shared a flat with a drama student, whom Janet didn't much care for.

'Oh yes. Steve's at college. I promise to behave, though.' He grinned at her infectiously.

'That wasn't quite what I meant, but I'm glad to hear it anyway. Go on then, you'll catch pneumonia. I'll see you later.'

'See you then, love,' he said, kissed her quickly on the cheek, and was gone.

Janet went back to polishing the glasses, and her musings. What had he said? *Pride and Prejudice?* Hadn't she seen a film of that ages ago? Oh no, that was *The Pride and the Passion.* May lead to big things, eh? Like what? Films? Why not, it had happened before. He might really become famous – and then what of her? She felt she was being left behind. If he did become really famous and rich, what would happen to their relationship? Little Miss Nobody from the backwoods was all right for a bit-part actor nobody had ever heard of, but if Roger became a big name, he'd want a consort to match. Somebody like – she had to admit it – Stephanie Sayers, somebody really beautiful and stylish that he could show off.

'She's one of those women who look better with their make-up off than on' was how he'd described her. And even with it on, it wouldn't be the sort of make-up Janet wore, a little bit of eye-shadow and mascara – it would be the full works, like those paralysing girls one saw round Oxford Circus at lunch-time. It was a different world altogether, one where she wouldn't fit in, and wouldn't even want to.

She gave herself a little shake. It hasn't happened yet, she told herself sternly, and it may never happen. And anyway, would you stand in his way? Of course not, was the only answer to that. Besides, if he loved her, it wouldn't make any difference how famous he was; and she did believe he loved her. He hadn't sounded in the least excited about Stephanie Sayers. And what was his first reaction when he heard the news? Didn't he come straight out in the rain with no coat on to tell her, Janet Anderson? Of course he did. And didn't he ask her to come round and help him with his script? Of course he did. So now, silly girl, what are you worried about?

She went round to his small, slummy flat after work, and when he had fed her on omelette and chips, they did some work on his script together. It was her evening off, so they worked until about seven, and then she cooked another meal, and they sat on the sofa and talked. He kissed her now and then, and seemed inclined to go further with her than he ever had before. She pushed him away, but didn't make too much of it. After all, it was his first big breakthrough, and he was naturally excited, but she hoped he wouldn't become too uppety, or she'd have to slap him down pretty hard. She had never let him get high and mighty with her, and she didn't intend to let him now, but just for this one evening she would let him brag a bit and be conceited. After pushing him away for the third time she said, 'Let's go to the cinema – I could fancy a film – I haven't been since that time with Vicky.'

'O.K., if you want to,' he said easily. 'What do you want to see?'

'They've got *Butch Cassidy* on at the Gaumont – I wouldn't mind seeing that again,' she said at random.

'A woman's film that – still I don't mind indulging you, just this once. Don't expect it every time though.'

And if I didn't think he was joking, so help me I'd plant him, Janet thought to herself grimly.

'Come on, horrible,' she said. 'Before your head gets so big we have to get a carpenter to let you out of the door.'

He laughed and put his arm round her shoulder, and her worry eased, for it was as natural a gesture as could be wished for. 'I don't know what you'd do without me to keep you human,' Janet said.

'I don't know either,' Roger said.

Janet's worst fears weren't realized as the weeks went by, for though she didn't see Roger quite so often, when she did see him he was just the same with her, as ordinary and friendly as he had ever been, and if he did occasionally boast a little he was still as ready to laugh at himself for it, when she pointed it out. A couple of weeks after he told her the news, he took her, on her day off, to watch a rehearsal, and there she first met 'The Opposition' as she thought of Stephanie Sayers.

She was even more beautiful than she had looked in the play Janet had seen her in. Her hair, which Roger had described as fair-mouse was an odd kind of silvery colour that was very attractive. Her fair skin and big blue eyes made her look a very English type of beauty, and she was tall, and though, when Janet saw her at rehearsal, she was dressed casually, in camel-coloured slacks and a peacock-blue jumper, she looked impeccably elegant. Janet felt a twinge when she saw her. Janet knew herself to be prettier than the average girl, and she had had lots of boy-friends ever since she was about fourteen, so she could hardly doubt she was attractive, but this woman had something Janet knew she could never emulate, a kind of rich sheen, an elegance, a grace that put her in a different class altogether.

Roger introduced them, and Stephanie Sayers shook hands in a perfectly natural way and said 'How do you do' and smiled, but she wasn't the least bit interested in Janet, and Janet had to say fairly to herself, why on earth should she be? Roger then introduced her to some of the other actors, and to two girls younger than herself who were playing the youngest

Bennett sisters (Janet had now read the book and was *au fait* with all the names) and Janet for the first time felt a little envy, and wished she could have been one of them.

Then the director called them all to order, and the rehearsal began. It was all very bitty at first, and if Janet hadn't had a vested interest in Roger she would have found it rather boring. She loved to hear Stephanie Sayers and Roger being catty to each other in their characters, and felt that they had both been well cast, for they seemed to fit the parts perfectly. After a while she got so involved in the proceedings that she quite forgot she was not an audience in a real theatre, and was quite shocked when Roger came over to her and asked if she would go to the shop across the road and get some sandwiches for them.

When she returned she found one of the young girls sitting in the seat next to hers, and she smiled at her as she sat down. After a while the girl said to her, 'Have you been going out with Roger long?'

'Since September – why?'

'I just wondered,' the girl said, and then went pink. 'I'm crazy about him,' she said, giggling nervously. 'I've had a crush on him for ages, and when they told me I'd got this part, I was thrilled to bits, and then he brought you along. I could have murdered you.' She said it without rancour. 'You are lucky! How did you meet him?'

'In a pub,' Janet said. 'I'm a barmaid.'

'A barmaid? Are you really? That must be fun,' the girl said.

'I was thinking the same about your job.'

'Well, I like it, of course, but you get pushed around an awful lot. And you never get to meet people, the way you would as a barmaid.'

'I don't see what you mean. I mean, you've met all these people, haven't you?' Janet said, puzzled.

'Yes, but they don't take any notice of you. *You*'re Roger's girl-friend, after all. He hardly ever even says hello to me.'

There it was, thought Janet. There's always someone who thinks you're the luckiest person on God's earth. Here was this kid green with envy and having a crush on Roger – Janet looked at Roger with a stranger's eyes for the first time in ages. He was stunningly handsome, and in the part of Darcy he was also sophisticated, elegant, a man of the world. She felt her pulse quicken. She did love him, though it had taken a long time for her to find it out, and maybe it was the danger of losing him that was bringing it home to her sharply. Elizabeth Bennett made a scornful rejoinder to him, and he parried it neatly, and despite the overt dislike between them, one could feel that they were really bound to come together in the end; they were so clearly made for each other, both so handsome, witty, intelligent —

The rehearsal broke, and Roger came over to her, stooping to kiss her forehead.

'How was I?' he asked.

'Stunning,' she said. 'It's not your acting though – it was simply type-casting so you couldn't really fail, could you?'

'Don't be nasty. Come on, I'll take you for a drink.'

'Where?' Janet asked suspiciously.

'Over the road, where the others go.'

'Couldn't we go somewhere else? I want to be alone with you.'

'Now she tells me! That'll have to wait till later, my love. I have to be back in an hour for a private session, so I can't take you far.'

'Oh, all right then. Come on, let's go.'

'You really are anxious to get me away by myself, aren't you?' Roger said, half laughing, half mystified. If only you knew, Janet thought.

The weeks rolled on towards Christmas, and things didn't change much, except that Janet saw less of Roger, and felt restless in her job, wanting a change. She decided that after Christmas she would get a different job, perhaps in an office, or maybe at the B.B.C. – Andy had said that he could get her in. She had seen him once or twice recently, when Roger was rehearsing during her free times and, at a loose end, she had gone up to the Centre bar for something to do. Andy had congratulated her on Roger's success and had asked her in what Janet thought was a pointed manner, who was playing

Lizzy Bennett. She wasn't sure afterwards if she had imagined it, but she felt she detected a note of sympathy in Andy's voice when she told him who it was.

She was in Roger's flat one Sunday afternoon, curled up on the sofa listening to records and sipping a martini – Roger had more money now, and was beginning to live like a 'star', which sometimes amused and sometimes annoyed Janet, when the subject of Christmas came up.

'What're you doing for Christmas, anyway?' Roger asked her.

'I'm going home – taking the whole week off for it. Why?'

'Oh, nothing.' Roger sounded disappointed.

'Where are you going?'

'I'm going home to my parents' house. I haven't been back for Christmas for years. I was rather hoping you'd come too.'

'Oh, I'm sorry,' Janet said, genuinely disappointed. 'I'd have liked that – but I've arranged it all now. And I haven't seen my parents since I came down. I kept promising to go up for a weekend, but I could never make it, and they're so looking forward to me coming home – I couldn't disappoint them.'

'All right,' he said crossly. 'You don't have to go on about it. I understand.'

'Don't snap at me like that,' she said reasonably. 'How should I have known you wanted me to spend Christmas with your folks? You never mentioned it.'

'No, I didn't think of it until quite recently. I sort of took it for granted you'd spend Christmas with me. I forgot you have a family.' He put a funny kind of emphasis on 'family' as if it were rather an infra-dig thing to have, and it was on the tip of her tongue to ask him if Stephanie had a family, but she couldn't quite be that bitchy. Besides, he had wanted her for Christmas, and seemed upset that she would be going away. She stroked his hair, and he swung himself round on the sofa and lay down across her lap. 'Never mind,' he said, 'it doesn't matter.'

She bent her head and kissed him.

'I don't know if I like the sound of that. It sounds a bit final,' she said.

'Eh?' he said vaguely, as if he hadn't been listening, and

kissed her again.

'Careful, you'll make me spill my drink,' she said.

'Put your glass down, then,' he said, and took it out of her hand. After a while she drew breath to say, 'Will you still go down to see them?'

'Who?' he asked.

'Your folks? At Christmas I mean?'

'Oh, I don't know. I expect so.'

'I think Christmas is a time to be with your family, don't you think?'

'Mm.' His mind wasn't on it.

Steve came barging in and broke it up.

'Oh sorry, didn't know you'd be at it,' he said loudly and rudely. He stamped over to the television and turned it on, and sat down in the chair beside it. Roger raised his eyebrows expressively at Janet, and then said, 'I wouldn't mind a bit of privacy, you know.'

'What? Well, why on earth do it here then? If you want privacy you should use the bedroom. Or why don't you go to her flat?'

'Don't be a bore, Steve,' Roger said more sharply. 'You only do it to annoy.'

'Well if you don't like it, you know what to do,' said the other immovably. 'You won't be here much longer anyway.'

'What d'you mean?'

'Well you're getting far too important and rich to stay in a slum like this, aren't you? And when you move out, it'll be my flat, so I may as well have the run of it now. Why bother with the technicalities?'

'Look, allow me to decide when I move. And I'm hardly rich yet, and not likely to be in the near future,' Roger said.

Steve turned round with a grin.

'Modest! Haven't you told her about those two offers you've had? One from the I.T.V. —'

'How did you know about those?' Roger interrupted.

'You leave your letters lying about,' Steve said simply. 'You're on to a good thing there, Janet – he's quite the up and coming boy.'

'C'mon, Jan, we'll get no peace here – let's go out,' Roger

said, and she, not liking Steve in this mood any more than he did, got up obediently. They set off in the general direction of Janet's flat, though without discussing a destination.

'Is that true?' she asked him after a silent walk of some minutes.

'They're only tentative offers,' Roger said, following her drift. 'Would I like to be considered for ... that sort of thing.'

She was silent a moment.

'Then you might become famous after all?'

'What do you mean, after all? Didn't you always believe I'd be the tops?' he asked, and it was only half a joke.

'It never even entered my mind,' she said, and he laughed and changed the subject.

CHAPTER ELEVEN

Janet found that she was next thing to a celebrity when she finally got home. Her parents had seen the man in question on the television, and thought him a decent sort of chap, and Sylvia was quite wild with envy that Janet had had that sort of luck on her very first trip into the big wide world. On Christmas Eve Vicky arranged a booze-up with some of the people from work at which Janet was the guest of honour, and she had to tell over and over again what it was like to go out with a telly-star, what it was like inside the studios, and answered again and again the question, was London really like they said?

She was glad, though, to get away from the hustle and noise and general jollity back to the quietness of her home, and her own little bedroom that she had slept in almost since she was born. Everything was the same, but it all looked different to her, which was what made her realize that she had changed in the four months she had been away. She escaped the preliminary festivities downstairs and went up to her room and shut the door, and sitting on the floor she took out of the bottom of her wardrobe a cardboard shoe-box, rather soft and tatty at the edges, held shut with a rubber band. Her Treasure Box, she used to call it. She slipped off the band, took the lid off, and began slowly to sort through the treasures.

The programme from the school play that her school had done with the co-operation of the neighbouring boys' school. There under the cast list was her name: 'Ladies in Waiting ... Sarah Smith, Jane Hobbs, Janet Anderson'. And there, at the back, was the blurred photograph of the boy who played the lead part in the play, Derek Warren, her first heart-throb. She had had a terrible crush on him at the age of fourteen, and had gone to all the rehearsals, even the ones she didn't have to go to, so that she could stare moonily and (unknown to her until afterwards) drive him scatty with it. She rummaged in the bottom of the box and dug up a fragment of a stick of

113

grease-paint, No. 5, which had been his, and which she had filched off the school-desk in the green-room that he had used as his dressing-table, just after his entrance in the second act.

She gave a little smile to herself, and remembered the days when the crush had been at its worst, when she had sneaked up here to her bedroom just to take out this little No. 5 stick and hold it, for comfort.

A bus ticket . . . that was from the time she had gone with Jane Hobbs and Pete Daly and Morris Cawshaw on the bus up to Archer's Mill. Morris had been in love with her, and the four of them had played hookey one afternoon from school and gone up the Mill on the bus. They'd gone swimming in the Mill pond in their underwear, and Morris had kissed her in the water, and Jane and Pete climbed up into the ruined mill and got covered in cobwebs and lichen. That was how they'd been found out. They'd all got into trouble over that, but it had been worth it.

Photographs – the little photos you get in those machines on railway stations or in Woolworths. Four of her, looking like a convict. One of her crushed up against Morris, grinning. One of Morris on his own, serious. One of Jane and Pete pretending to kiss but looking hard at the camera all the same. A proper studio photo of a sleekly handsome blond boy with 'Yours, Ekki' written across the corner. That was from their holiday in Austria.

Letters – some from old girl-friends, some from boys. She turned them over, but didn't read them. She knew every word of every one off by heart. A dud bullet and a foreign coin with a hole in the middle. They were from Arthur, the soldier, who had taken her out for two weeks on his long leave, and then gone back to Germany. One of the letters there was from him. Only one.

Funny how she had taken care of all this junk, hidden it in the wardrobe, preserved it all in secret. It had been so important to her, even up to the time she had gone away to London. Now – she could throw it in the bin outside and not blink an eyelid at it. She felt very sad, and she hardly knew why. Perhaps she was growing up at last – though she was old enough, she should have done it years ago.

114

The door opened softly and closed again. Janet looked up and saw Sylvia standing there, looking at her uncertainly.

'Janet, love —' she hesitated. 'Is there anything wrong? You've been awful quiet, I wondered if anything had happened.'

'Oh, not really,' Janet said. 'At least, nothing I could put a name to.'

'It isn't your young man is it?' Sylvia asked, not convinced. Janet looked at her for a long moment – Sylvia, so pretty, so content, never having doubted for a moment what her life was all about.

'I suppose it is, in a way,' she said reluctantly, and then a moment later she told her sister the whole story. Sylvia listened in silence, and then stared thoughtfully at the box Janet still held without seeing it.

'Well, I don't know,' she said at last. 'It seems to me that he hasn't said or done anything wrong, or even different since he's got this part. It seems to me that the difference is all on your side. Are you sure you aren't making up troubles for yourself, because you've got an inferiority complex about this Stephanie person?'

'I know it sounds like that, Syl, but it isn't really. It isn't anything you can really put your finger on, but just now and again he comes out with something – he isn't the same boy I started to go out with.'

'Well I suppose he couldn't be really, could he? But can't you change with him?'

'Not if he really hits the big time,' Janet said a little bitterly.

'But he hasn't yet. Why borrow trouble? Come down and join in the fun, and forget all about it for a while. Mum and Dad will be upset if you spoil their Christmas for them, when they've looked forward to it for so long.'

'Are you girls comin' down?' their father's voice called up at that moment. 'We're just goin' to dress t' tree.'

'Coming, Dad!' Sylvia called back. She looked at Janet, smiling, and Janet had to agree with her.

'All right, I'll come,' she said. She stood up, and noticed she was still holding her treasure box. She glanced down at it, and then put the rubber band back on, and carried it down with her, taking a moment to slip out the back, through the kitchen, and drop it into the bin.

Janet made up her mind to forget about her problems over Christmas, and on the whole she stuck to her resolution. Everything was done in traditional style at home, dressing the tree, Midnight Mass, then on Christmas Morning the presents, then Christmas dinner with all the trimmings, and a long sit over the port and nuts to talk. Then they went for the Christmas walk, down to the canal and back, and Janet and Sylvia took bread with them and fed the ducks. They were very tame this year, perhaps because it had turned very cold, and actually came up and took bread from their hands. Janet was nervous at first that they would peck her fingers, but she discovered that their beaks were light, almost like thin plastic, and even when they did get hold of a finger by mistake it didn't hurt. It made her feel that she and Sylvia were kids again, despite the presence of Geoff and baby Neville – they might almost have been brothers. Sylvia certainly looked young enough, with her cheeks rosy and her eyes shining from the cold, and when she took Neville and stood him on his feet and gave him bread to hold out to the ducks, she looked almost too young to be his mother.

Looking at them, Janet felt a sudden pang. Why had she fallen in love with an actor of all people? What she really wanted was to be settled and easy, like Syl and Geoff, and to be ordinary and have a baby like other girls. She had gone to London in search of excitement and something different, but she would have been better advised to stay at home, for what she really needed was here after all. Still, it was too late to turn back now. She was in love with Roger, for better or worse. For better or worse – the marriage service – Roger had never mentioned marriage, nor even engagement; but he had wanted to take her to meet his parents at Christmas, and that looked like a serious sort of intention. She wondered if he had gone after all – he hadn't sounded terribly keen when she last mentioned it. She caught Sylvia's eye and forced herself to smile and forget Roger again.

When they got back she and Sylvia insisted that Mum put

her feet up, for she had been on the go since she got up that morning, and Dad and Geoff took her into the sitting room to talk and play some records of dance-music, which was Mum's favourite, though she didn't often get time to sit down and listen, while Janet and Sylvia went into the kitchen to get tea. With the kettle on and quietly singing, and the two girls side by side at the table cutting bread and making turkey sandwiches it was an ideal time to talk.

'You're still miserable, aren't you, Jan?' Sylvia began.

'I am trying, Syl, honestly,' Janet said. 'It's a bit strong to say I'm miserable though – I'm not really miserable, just uncertain.'

'You really do love this fella then?'

'Yes, I suppose I do. I didn't mean to, but it seems to have crept up on me.'

'And do you think he loves you?'

'I really don't know. I think so most of the time, but he's never actually mentioned marriage, unless you count inviting me home at Christmas.'

'You didn't tell me about that,' Sylvia said, surprised.

'Didn't I? He asked me to go with him to his parents' house, but of course I'd already arranged to come here, so I couldn't.'

'Well, that certainly sounds as if he's serious about you,' Sylvia said.

'D'you think so?'

'Of course – you don't introduce people to your family if you aren't pretty far gone on them. Why, don't you think so?'

'I don't know,' Janet said, frowning into the distance and absently twiddling the knife she was holding. 'Sometimes he's very ordinary, just like any of the boys we used to knock about with. But sometimes he behaves like an actor, and you just never know with people like that what's going on in their heads.'

'I see. Well, if I were you, I should have it out with him when you get back, find out where you stand.'

'I couldn't possibly!' Janet exclaimed. 'I can't just ask him out of the blue if he's going to marry me.'

'I don't see why not,' Sylvia said briskly. 'I had to do it with

117

Geoff. Young men never know they want to get married until you put it into their heads. Find out which way the wind's blowing, and then if he isn't as serious about you as you thought, you'll just have to be sensible about it and try and forget him.' Sylvia said all this without looking at Janet, but now she left off buttering bread and gave her sister a sympathetic look. 'Don't worry too much. From what you tell me I'm sure he loves you. He's just a bit thoughtless, that's all.'

Janet forced a smile. 'Thanks, I expect you're right. If there is anything wrong I think it's my fault. I seem to be becoming a nasty person these days. Jealous I suppose. Poor Rodge!'

'That's better, that's more like my Janet,' Sylvia said, sounding relieved. 'Kettle's boiling. Shall you make the tea, then?'

The rest of the Christmas week passed quietly. There wasn't much to do during the day, for most people went back to work on the twenty-seventh, and she found herself growing bored, and wanting to be back in London. In the evenings she went to see old friends, but now that the newness of her return had worn off she was no longer feted, and those evenings out tended to become 'shop' conversations, for nearly everyone worked at Emersons, or at the Louth Mills, and the talk about office scandals, and who was going out with whom, and how-I-stood-up-to-Mr.-So-and-so reminded her of why, in the first place, she had taken the plunge and gone to London. At the end of the week she had had quite enough, and decided to go back a day early, on Saturday, so that she could have Sunday to unpack and bath and so on, and incidentally to have a lunchtime drink in one of her favourite pubs and perhaps even see Roger.

Mum and Dad were sorry to say goodbye to her, and asked her repeatedly to write, and to come up for weekends, but Janet only felt a lifting of her heart as the train pulled out of the station and picked up speed, hurtling south through the black-and-grey countryside. She imagined her little room in the scruffy old house and the kitchen where she sat in the mornings over her cup of coffee listening to the transistor radio, and the cheerful, noisy market on a Saturday afternoon, and 'The Sun in Splendour' on a Sunday lunchtime, and Mary

118

and her customers at the pub, and she knew that, even without bringing Roger into it, she was glad to be going back. Her trip home had taught her that much, at least.

It was nearly nine o'clock when she reached the house and, taking her key out of her handbag, climbed the dark smelly stairs to the top floor. She was surprised and perturbed to hear the sound of crying from inside, which stopped as she opened the front door, and then went on again louder than before. She shut the door, put her bags and coat in her room, and then went along the passage to the sitting room from where the crying was coming.

Janet stopped at the door, and saw Sandra sitting on the floor with her arms on the seat of the sofa and her head in her arms, sobbing loudly. A little pile of soggy tissues beside her on the sofa told of how long she had been at it.

'What's up, Sandy? What is it?' Janet asked anxiously, though she had an odd feeling she knew already. She crouched down beside Sandra and put a hand on her shoulder, uncertain what to do. At first Sandra would only cry the louder but eventually when Janet asked for the third or fourth time what was the matter, the other girl said indistinctly, 'It's Dick. I've broken off with him.'

'Why? What's happened?' Janet asked.

'He's been going out with another girl all this time.'

Bit by bit Janet got the whole story out of her. Sandra and Dick had arranged to go out on Saturday evening for a meal, but Dick had called her at short notice to say that he couldn't make it, and that he'd been called to an extra rehearsal. Sandra, covering up her dignity, had said that was all right, she had wanted to wash her hair anyway. Her hair didn't actually need washing, and feeling bored she had decided to go up to the B.B.C. club for a drink, hoping that some friends would be there. As she arrived at the door she had met Dick coming out with a girl of their mutual acquaintance on his arm. There had followed a somewhat undignified and acrimonious exchange, and Sandra had fled home to weep.

Janet made the right sort of comforting noises, and hoisted Sandra off the floor and into the kitchen where she sat her at the table while she made some coffee for them both. It seemed strange that Sandra, who had always considered herself older and wiser than Janet and had often given advice about affairs of the heart to the other girl, should be the one to be receiving comfort for the very affliction she had warned about. But still, it was a kind of hopeful sign for her, Janet thought, for it would be too much of a coincidence if the same thing happened to her, so she could pretty much rely that it wouldn't.

She continued to act the good Samaritan on Sunday by taking Sandra with her for a lunchtime drink. They went to the 'Kensington' to listen to the jazz, and met a few of Janet's acquaintances, among them a very good-looking young man who appeared to be smitten with Sandra, who cheered up a lot and allowed him to buy her three Camparis. By the time they wandered out of the pub into the freezing air, Sandra had arranged to meet him that night for a drink, and Janet thought drily, now perhaps I can concentrate on my own evening's plans.

When she got home she dialled the number of Roger's flat. She didn't know if he had gone away, or if he had come back yet, but it was worth a try – she longed to see him. It rang for a long time, and just when she was about to put the receiver down it was answered.

'Hello?' Janet was disappointed – it was Steve's voice.

'Hello, is Roger there?' There was a curious sort of hesitation, and then Steve said, 'Is that Janet?'

'Yes,' she said, and feeling oddly nervous gabbled on. 'I suppose he isn't back yet. I didn't know what day he was coming back, but I thought I'd try. That is,' she remembered, 'if he went away.'

'Where?' Steve asked, sounding vague.

'Home, to his parents. Why, didn't he go after all?'

'Oh, yes, he went all right.'

'And is he back?'

'Er, no – no, he isn't back. I don't know what day he's coming back, but when he arrives I'll tell him you phoned. Is there a message?'

'No, just to contact me, that's all,' Janet said in a flat voice.

'O.K.,' Steve said, and put the phone down, without another

120

word. Janet put the receiver down slowly, feeling oddly dissatisfied with the whole conversation. Pity he wasn't back. She'd just have to find something else to do. After a moment she decided to go to the Club. At least Andy would be there – he always was on Sunday evenings – and he would be company for her. Yes, that's what she would do.

She didn't think about it, but if she had it might have been interesting to discover what were the subconscious promptings that made her dress extra carefully and extra attractively that evening.

CHAPTER TWELVE

The club was quite crowded when Janet arrived, but she was still able to locate Andy immediately by the noise that came from the group of which he was the centre. She threaded her way through to them, and was greeted by Andy with a heartiness that cheered her.

'Janet my angel, how lovely to see you again. You look divine! Come here, I must give you a kiss for Christmas, not to mention New Year.'

She went over to him and let him put his arm round her shoulder, and she turned her cheek up to him for his kiss. He kissed the middle of her cheek loudly, and then said, 'Well, a chaste kiss like that's all right for Christmas, I suppose – must keep all pure for the kiddies' sakes – but New Year is a pagan festival, and I want a proper kiss for that.'

Much as she liked Andy she didn't much want to kiss him on the mouth, and she said, 'Then you must wait until the New Year for it – no queue-jumping.'

'There's only a few hours to go – don't be so technical,' Andy objected, and Janet stared at him in astonishment.

'It isn't New Year's Eve is it?'

'Of course it is. That's why all these people are here.' That explained why it was so crowded, Janet thought, but she said nothing, and Andy went on instructively. 'You will find that it is a common phenomenon in this country, that New Year's Eve always falls on the same day as Christmas Eve and exactly a week later. No-one has ever been able to explain why this is so, but it's never been known to fail.' Janet was still staring at him as if in amazement, so he took the opportunity to kiss her, and she wasn't quick enough to avoid it.

'Thanks,' he said, smiling, and Janet had to smile back. 'Now what would you like to drink?'

'I'd like – a – Campari and lemonade,' she said on an impulse. It sounded sophisticated, and she suddenly wanted to be

122

sophisticated. She wanted to be elegant and smart and witty and cruel like the fashionable girls, like the heroines in novels who had hoards of men trailing after them, so many they got bored with them.

'Whatever you like,' Andy said, detecting a slight note of enquiry in her voice. 'I see Christmas boozing has affected your tastes. No more simple pints for you. You're jaded, you need stimulation. Campari and lemonade it shall be.'

When the drink came, it tasted pretty awful to her, like after-shave or hair tonic or something, but she couldn't admit why she asked for it so she had to pretend to like it, and after the third the pretence was almost a reality. Everyone was in great good humour, and the jokes and quips were flying thick and fast. Janet joined in as well as anyone, and she and Andy made a kind of double-act, setting each other off and providing each other's cues, like a kind of Morecambe and Wise, and kept the company laughing. The Camparis went to her head, and she felt quite happy, and didn't even mind the odd looks that Andy was giving her now and again.

Just before midnight everyone quietened down, and the radio was switched on behind the bar so that everyone could hear the chimes of Big Ben. There was a hushed silence, and then the familiar chime rang out, and there was a great cheer, as if the company had only one voice between them. Then began the usual round of kissing and back-slapping and wishing happy New Year to friends and strangers alike, and people began to join hands to sing Auld Lang Syne.

Janet had moved quite a way from her original company by this time, and had kissed and been kissed so often she had lost count. She found her arm, however, firmly grasped by Andy, and as they reeled backwards and forwards with the rest to the tuneless roaring of the old song, she felt that there was something of disapproval in the way he was looking at her. At last the party began to break up as the bar staff tried to hustle people away, and Andy took a firm grip of Janet and said, 'I'll see you home. We'll get a taxi.'

'That's very kind of you, but it isn't necessary,' Janet began, trying to be dignified.

'It is necessary. You shouldn't drink things you aren't used to in such quantities.'

Janet laughed.

'That's the nicest way I've ever heard of telling someone she's drunk.'

'Oh, I don't think you're drunk. But I still want to talk to you,' Andy said.

He waited until they were in the taxi and speeding away through the quiet streets before he said, 'Now then! What's wrong with you and Roger?'

'What do you mean, what's wrong?' Janet asked.

'I mean, when a girl has been going about with a man she's obviously very fond of, and when she turns up alone on New Year's Eve and tries to get herself drunk in mixed – very mixed – company, then one is justified in thinking that there's something wrong.'

'Well, Sherlock Holmes, there's one explanation you haven't thought of.'

'What's that?'

'Supposing the man is away, out of town, and she misses him?'

Andy stared at her for a moment, and then said quietly, 'Why do you say that?'

'Say what?' Janet was puzzled.

'I mean, who told you that he was out of town?'

'His flat-mate, Steve. Besides, Roger told me before Christmas that he was going to spend it with his parents, so I knew he was going away. And when I phoned this afternoon, Steve said he wasn't back yet. That's why I came down here. Now are you satisfied?'

Janet was not absolutely drunk, but she had drunk enough to make her a little slow on the uptake, otherwise she might have gathered more from Andy's expression. He didn't say anything more until they drew up in front of the house, and then he said, 'Listen, Jan, can I come in for a minute? I want to talk to you.'

'Do you want a cup of coffee?' Janet asked him.

'Not particularly,' he said.

'That's good,' Janet said. 'Then you can come up.'

'What are you talking about?' Andy asked, frowning.

'Well, I've learnt that when a man says he wants to come up for a cup of coffee, that's about the only thing he doesn't want.'

That at least made him laugh, but by the time he'd paid off the taxi and they'd climbed the stairs to the flat, he was serious again. Sandra wasn't back yet. They went into the kitchen, and, for something to do, Janet put the kettle on and got mugs down from the cupboard. Then she sat down opposite Andy and gave him her attention.

'Look, Janet, I have to talk to you. I'm very fond of you – you know that –'

Janet nodded, blushing. It sounded like the beginning of a proposal of marriage.

'And I don't want to upset you, and I don't expect I'd be thanked for it either, but someone isn't playing straight with you, and you ought to know.'

'All this sounds very impressive,' Janet said, 'and very mysterious. What is it you want to say?' She had a feeling she already knew, and that made her speak more sharply than she would have otherwise.

'Try not to blame me too much,' Andy said, noting her ill-humour. 'I'll come to the point. You say that Roger went to stay with his parents over Christmas, and that he isn't back yet. I say he is back, as far as I know he never went.'

'Carry on,' said Janet calmly. She knew what was coming.

'He was in the club bar on Christmas Eve. I saw him twice during the week at the "York". And I saw him in the club bar again at lunchtime today – or rather yesterday as it now is.'

'I see,' Janet said, still calmly. 'Go on.'

Andy looked very serious, and seemed to hesitate, so she prompted him.

'What you want to say next is, he wasn't alone, isn't it?'

Andy nodded. 'You knew then?'

'I guessed. I could tell from your expression. I suppose you want to tell me who it was?'

'You know that too, don't you?'

'Stephanie Sayers.' Andy nodded. 'The kettle's boiling,' Janet said automatically and stood up to turn it off. She made two mugs of coffee and brought them back to the table, sat

125

down, and pushed the sugar towards Andy. He seemed disconcerted by her calmness. At last she said, 'Now, you don't need to look so funeral about it. After all, the only person who's deceived me is his flat-mate, Steve. Steve never liked me, and I expect he did it out of spite, to make trouble between me and Roger.'

'But —' Andy began to protest, but Janet cut him short.

'No, don't you see, there could be any number of explanations. Roger said he was going away, but he could easily have changed his mind after I'd already left. There may have been extra rehearsals called or something. And naturally he'd go out for drinks with the cast if he was working over Christmas and I wasn't there. So don't worry any more.'

'Whatever you say,' Andy said, shrugging.

'I understand why you wanted to tell me, and I'm grateful for your concern,' Janet said, and that was the end of it. Andy drank his coffee and said he'd better be going, and Janet went to the door with him, and as he was about to leave, on an impulse she kissed his cheek and thanked him again. He turned to her and said, 'If you need me at all, you know where I'm to be found.'

'I'll remember,' she said lightly. 'Goodnight.'

She was touched that he felt so much concern for her, and while one half of her mind laughed and told her that he was upset over nothing, the other half said that he wouldn't be so upset if there wasn't cause. But she wouldn't allow herself to speculate over what Andy had seen or thought he had seen. She would wait for Roger to contact her and let him tell her all about it. Until then she would trust him.

She had to wait a long time, and it wasn't easy. She went back to work on New Year's Day, and wasn't sorry to be back with the familiar faces and the familiar tasks, even the familiar smells, but it was very quiet in the aftermath of the festive season; only the regulars came in, and everyone seemed to be suffering from the anti-climax and tended to be grumpy and discontented. Only Mary remained serene and untroubled, passing the same remarks with the same customers every day and never seeming to notice if anyone spoke shortly to her.

126

Before Christmas Janet had been restless and thinking about a change of job, but now she found she was content here, and, more, needed the security of the place and the people. How much of that was due to her uncertainty over Roger she didn't know, and didn't care to find out. She was sore and angry inside that he took so long to contact her. She could have telephoned him, but she didn't, pride telling her that she had made the first move, and now it was up to him. Since it was quiet, Stan set them all to a kind of New-Year-cleaning, and that kept them busy. Walls and curtains were washed, upholstery cleaned, everything taken off the shelves and the shelves washed and the mirrors polished. Janet took an old knife to the underside of the counter, her special bug-bear, and stripped off the toffee-like accumulation of beer-spillings, and then washed it with disinfectant-water. New towels and dish-cloths were bought, and everyone felt better for the turning out.

At last, on the Wednesday ten days after New Year, Roger appeared during the morning session. He walked in and stood just inside the door watching her as she was serving a customer, and it was like that that she first saw him when she looked up from what she was doing. Her heart seemed to miss a beat, and she realized in that moment as never before how much she loved him, how much she had missed him. She had deliberately tried not to think of him, and had almost forgotten what he looked like, but now she felt the blood rushing to her cheeks, and a thrill ran through her as he smiled at her in the old way and came forward to an empty part of the bar.

She walked across to meet him, and he reached his hands across the bar and took hers and held them as he gazed into her face, smiling all the time that dazzling smile.

'Hello Jan,' he said softly. 'Happy New Year!' He leaned forward to kiss her, but his words reminded her of how long she had been neglected, and she stiffened.

'New Year was ages ago,' she said. He pressed her hands and smiled with a charming air of apology.

'I know, I've been neglecting you, poor darling. I've been so busy, you wouldn't believe. This is literally the first chance I've had to see you.'

'You could have phoned,' she said, beginning to yield in spite of herself.

'I never seemed to be free at the times you would be home, and I didn't like to phone here. I wasn't sure how the governor would take to it. You aren't really angry with me, are you?'

'I suppose not,' Janet said, weakening. He pressed her hands, and she said, 'No, I'm not angry.'

'Give me a New Year kiss then, to show you've forgiven me.'

She leaned forward and kissed him, and felt her inside fluttering at the contact. Then she pulled away.

'That's enough for now, or I'll be losing my job. Are you drinking?'

'Oh, just a light ale for now. What about you?'

'I'll have a coke, thanks. I don't feel like booze.'

She fetched the drinks and rang up the money, served a customer, and then came back to Roger.

'Did you have a nice Christmas, then?' he asked her. 'Tell me all about it.'

'It was very quiet,' she said. 'Just a sort of family Christmas, you know, the tree and the turkey and all the usual things.'

'Did you go out at all?'

'A couple of times, with the old gang, but it was very quiet. It always is at home – there's never anything to do.'

'Didn't you enjoy it, then?'

'Oh yes, in some ways. I liked the peace and quiet, but I was glad to get back here too. I missed the old place.'

'I know what you mean,' Roger said. Janet saw a customer with an empty glass looking at her, and she said, 'I must go and serve.'

'Oh, don't worry about me, I'll just read the paper. You carry on.'

She went to serve feeling rather uneasy. Perhaps it was because they hadn't seen each other for so long, but Roger didn't seem to be behaving naturally – he was too polite, as if she was a stranger. Perhaps he had a guilty conscience. She would bring the conversation around to his Christmas and give him the chance to tell her naturally. She glanced back at him, so heartbreakingly handsome, sitting on the high stool with his legs crossed and his dark head bent over the newspaper. She finished serving, rinsed a couple of glasses, and went back down the bar to Roger.

They chatted for a few minutes, and then, during a pause in the conversation, she said, trying to sound as casual as possible, 'What kind of a Christmas did you have? Did you go to your folks after all?'

'Oh, yes. It was pretty much like yours, really, only a bit more formal perhaps. Neighbours in for drinks on Christmas Eve, that sort of thing.'

Janet felt as if she had been struck a blow. She had never expected this. She said, in a voice so hesitant that he must have noticed it, 'You were down there for Christmas Eve then?'

'Oh yes, the whole thing. All the traditions. I decided to go the whole hog this year, since I haven't been to see them for so long.'

His laugh sounded loud and unnatural in her ears, she felt a little sick.

'What's the matter, Jan? You look a bit off-colour.' Roger's voice seemed to come from a long way away. His concern looked so genuine that she said after a moment, 'Can I see you at closing time?' She wanted to give him one last chance.

'Of course, that's what I intended. I'll take you for a bite to eat, and then we can go and sit on my sofa and talk nonsense for an hour or so.'

It all sounded so nearly normal that she wondered for a moment if she had been dreaming. She looked at her watch. It was a quarter to three, thank God. Only about half an hour to last out.

Roger watched her with concern in his face as she got through the last thirty minutes somehow. Once time had been called it was easier for her, for there were buckets to be emptied and glasses to be washed, ashtrays to be wiped and crates to be shifted, plenty for her to do to keep her occupied. At last everything was done and everyone was out, and she rinsed her hands under the tap, picked up her handbag, put her coat on, and nodded towards Roger, who was sitting at the bar waiting for her. They went out into the cold air and the grey world, and Janet turned to him.

'Can we go straight back to your place?' she asked. Roger put his arms round her waist and looked at her seriously for a moment. Then he kissed her forehead and said, 'All right. Come on then.' They didn't speak at all on the way there, and when they got in he took her coat and told her to sit by the fire and get warm while he rustled up something to eat. When he came in with plates of scrambled eggs on toast, tea, and swiss roll, he seemed normally cheerful, and setting the tray down he pushed her gently down again as she tried to stand up and said, 'Eat something first. You're hungry.'

He was right, she was hungry, and when she had eaten and was sipping her second cup of tea she acknowledged that she felt much better.

'Thanks Roger,' she said. 'I needed that.'

'That's all right,' he said, with a queer little gesture, almost like a salute. 'They call me the good Samaritan.' He looked at her for a moment, penetratingly, and then came over to sit beside her, put his arm round her, and kiss her. She allowed the first two, but turned her face away from his mouth.

'Roger,' she said, 'I know you didn't go to your parents' at Christmas.'

She hadn't meant to blurt it out, she had meant to trap him into admitting it, but she found that she had to play fair with him, even if he didn't with her.

'Go on,' he said quietly. She looked at him, and saw that he was serious, grave not angry.

'Someone I know saw you with Stephanie Sayers on several occasions while I was away.'

'Go on,' he said again.

'That's all,' she said.

'No, it isn't,' he said. 'You want me to explain it away – you don't believe the worst of me, you think there's an explanation.'

'How do you know that?' she asked.

'Because if you thought the worst of me, you wouldn't be here now, or at least you wouldn't be talking so calmly – you'd

130

be throwing things at me.' A tiny smile pulled at her lips despite herself. He smiled back at her, his blue eyes innocent, appealing. 'If I'd known you would be so generous about it, I wouldn't have told that silly lie in the first place. I'm glad you've found out, really I am. I hated the idea of deceit between us.'

'Then why did you?' she asked reasonably. He shrugged.

'Oh, it was silly, I know. You see, I didn't go to my parents' place when I planned to because of extra rehearsals being called for Stephanie and me. There were scenes between us that the director wasn't satisfied with, so we had to go in and work over Christmas, so as to keep up with the schedule. And quite naturally we went out for a drink together after we'd finished.'

Janet nodded. It seemed reasonable enough. 'But why did you say you went home? Why bother to lie?'

'I was stupid,' he said, holding his hands out in a gesture of despairing of himself. 'I thought you wouldn't understand, that you'd jump to the wrong conclusions and think that Stephanie and I were – well, you know. I should have known you better.'

'You should have,' she commented wrily. He took her chin in his hand and turned her face up to his. His eyes looked into hers, almost hypnotic at such close range.

'I'm sorry, darling, will you forgive me?' Without waiting for an answer he kissed her lips gently, then the tip of her nose, then her lips again, a long kiss this time that left her breathless. When he finally let her draw breath he whispered again, 'Forgive me?' and it went without saying that she had, though it was emotional rather than rational. She simply couldn't resist him.

CHAPTER THIRTEEN

Things settled down again, and for a month everything seemed to be back to normal. Sandra's New Year's Eve pick-up turned out to be very nice, and she was now going strong with him, and had apparently completely got over Richard Murray. Janet continued to see Roger at infrequent intervals, for they were actually filming now, which apparently took up even more of his time than rehearsing had, and apart from that he had auditioned for a couple of other parts, and had been approached about a commercial.

Things really did seem to be moving for him, and Janet had to be glad for him, since it was his chosen career, though it meant that she saw little of him, and that when she did see him he sometimes seemed to her to be an entirely different person. She sometimes protested against his conceit or his putting on of airs, but he seemed to be unsquashable, and only laughed at her protests. It disheartened her, but she loved him as steadily as ever, and hoped that it was a phase that he would come out of when the filming had finished.

He didn't take her to see any of the programmes being shot, so she had quite a lot of time on her hands, and she spent it in various ways; getting about London to see some of the famous sights, visiting art galleries and museums, playing darts in the local pubs, going to see Andy at the Centre. He was always glad to see her, and it gave her a feeling of being near Roger, however spurious it was.

It was her birthday at the beginning of February, and though she told herself that she was too old for birthdays to mean anything, she was disappointed when Roger told her he would have to work that night.

'I'd have loved to take you out somewhere, but I'm afraid it's not on. Still, I'll make up to you for it at the weekend. We'll have a special celebration. Would you like us to throw a party?'

'No, not really,' she said. 'Just a private celebration between you and me, that's what I'd like.'

'Whatever you say, love. It's your birthday.'

He might as well have said 'It's your funeral' she thought gloomily, and then she decided that even if he had to work, that didn't mean she had to sit indoors and mope. Andy would take her out somewhere. Good old Andy, the faithful standby! She felt a bit guilty sometimes about Andy, but after all she liked him, and he seemed to enjoy her company, so why not? He was old enough to object if he felt he was being used. She gave him a ring.

'I'd be delighted,' he said when she proposed celebrating her birthday with him. 'Where would you like to go?'

'I don't mind, as long as it's somewhere special, not the club. And, by the way, it's my treat.'

Andy protested, but she was firm. 'You tell me somewhere that's nice, and I'll book a table. Don't argue, it's my birthday.'

'All right,' he said, sounding as though he was shrugging. 'How about Romano's, in Calder Street?'

'What's it like?' Janet asked.

'Romantic and smoochy. And expensive.'

'That sounds just the job.'

It certainly was a far cry from the White City, she discovered when she arrived there on her birthday night. The very carpet seemed thick with money, the silent, gliding waiters oozed richness. She was glad Andy was with her, for she would never have had the nerve to come in here on her own.

'It's fantastic,' she whispered to him when they were seated. 'If the people at home could see me now!'

'What a nice unspoilt girl you are,' Andy grinned. 'Far too nice to be wasted on anyone but me.'

'How do you know this place?' she asked him to distract his attention from that line of thought.

'Oh, it's one of the haunts of the rich and famous. One of those places that doesn't get into the newspapers, fortunately, but film stars, musicians, politicians – even Royalty come here.'

'Really!' Janet was surprised. 'But in that case, why did they accept my booking? I'm not any of those things.' Andy laughed.

'You don't *have* to be rich or famous, silly. The general public doesn't know this place exists, so that's protection enough for them.'

Knowing that Andy did know as much about food and wine as he pretended to, she let him order for them both, and they had the most delicious meal she had ever eaten, accompanied by a wine that even she knew was a world away from the stuff you bought at the wine-mart on the corner. After the meal they had three or four cups of excellent coffee, and Andy had a brandy with his while Janet, self-indulgently, had Benedictine. As she drank the last sip of it, she sighed contentedly and said to Andy,

'That was the loveliest —' she broke off, and gave a little cry.

'What's up?' Andy asked, concerned, and then noticed that she was staring at something behind him. He glanced round and saw what it was — Stephanie Sayers, looking exquisitely beautiful in evening dress, was just being divested of a white fur cape by a waiter. Behind her, in dinner jacket, looking every inch a film star and fit to be her companion, was Roger Jowitt.

Andy reached out over the table to take Janet's hand — it was an instinctive movement, to protect her, and she took hold of him and whispered urgently, without once taking her eyes off the couple in the limelight, 'Andy, get me out of here. Don't let them see me.'

Thank God, he thought, she's sensible, and doesn't want to make a scene. Roger and his elegant partner were led forward to a table and sat down. Roger had his back to the door, and Stephanie seemed to have eyes for only him. Besides it was dimly lit in the restaurant, so it was not likely they would be seen leaving. Andy called the waiter and whispered to him. The bill was paid, the coats brought quietly, and with as little fuss as could possibly be made, they slipped out and up the steps into the West End street. They walked along briskly looking for a taxi, and picked one up quite soon, at the corner of the street. Inside Janet leaned back against the comforting leather and gave a long, shaky sigh. It was almost a sigh of relief. Andy took her hand, and she pressed his reassuringly.

'There's no explanation, is there?' she said.

'What do you mean?' Andy asked.

She told him what Roger had said about the times he had been seen at Christmas.

'I wondered why you went back with him,' Andy said. 'It certainly sounded reasonable.'

'But it can't be that way this time, can it? I mean, they were both in evening dress, so they must have planned it, mustn't they?' Andy was silent, not knowing what answer she wanted, and then said at last, 'Yes, they must have.'

Janet was quiet for a moment, and then said, 'I've been expecting it. It's almost a relief now it's come.' A silence. 'I'm sorry I thought badly of Steve.'

'Steve?'

'Roger's flat-mate. He was obviously only trying to keep things quiet, covering up for a friend. I'm sorry I thought ill of him now.'

Andy came closer to her in the dark and put an arm round her. She shivered, but did not object.

'You're very calm,' he said. 'I expected you to cry.'

'I told you, I've been expecting it,' Janet said. But that wasn't the reason. She couldn't cry in front of Andy, because that would be betraying Roger in some way, silly though it seemed. She would cry later, when she was alone, and no-one would ever know how much.

'What will you do?' Andy asked, sympathetically.

'I don't know,' she said. 'I just don't know.' But she did know — she was going home. She wanted to run back to her mother like a little child with a hurt to be made better. She thought suddenly of Mrs. Landon — was this what had happened to her, that made her come back? Was this how she had felt? Janet had thought that life in London was somehow more real than at home, that this was Real Life and the other just the shadow, but it wasn't. It was just colder, and Janet needed warmth. Why, even with all her talking about freedom, she had got herself into a nice cosy little hole here — at the pub —

as like to the one she had left as possible.

She got rid of Andy at the door as nicely as possible, thanking him for a lovely evening and for being so kind. She felt a bit guilty still, but decided she would write to him later, when it was all over. She said goodnight and closed the door, but instead of going straight to bed with an aspirin as he had suggested and as she had agreed to do, she got her suitcase down and began to pack. She would go tomorrow morning, by the first possible train. She didn't want to stay in London a minute longer than necessary. When she had packed her cases and put the overspill into two carrier bags, and written a letter to Stan, and a note for Sandra explaining everything (she had paid a month's rent in advance, of which there were three weeks left to run, so she felt no guilt on behalf of her flat-mate) she sat down to wait for morning. She couldn't have slept, even if she had wanted to, so she went into the kitchen and quietly made herself a pot of tea. As soon as the tubes were running she would go up to Euston and wait there for a train. She was in a kind of a panic, in case someone should try to stop her.

Now that was an odd idea, she thought to herself, and paused to pursue it. What was she really afraid of? Why, of seeing Roger again, of course. And at the thought of Roger, the long-overdue tears filled her eyes, and forced their way out, and she laid her head down on her arms and cried, just as she had found Sandra crying only a month ago.

CHAPTER FOURTEEN

Janet's arrival back home caused some consternation, for it was so sudden and unexpected, and moreover Janet wouldn't give any firm reason why she had left. She simply said she had got tired of it and wanted to come home, and when her mother pressed her and asked why she hadn't given warning, she simply shrugged. Sylvia guessed that it was something to do with Roger, and Janet's steady refusal to admit even that much gave rise to some sisterly anxieties on Sylvia's part, which of course were proved false in time. After a few days the household settled down again and nothing more was said, though there was much silent conjecture, and Mum tried not to notice when she heard Janet crying in the middle of the night.

Janet wrote to Andy, thanking him again for his kindness and explaining that she hadn't wanted to risk seeing Roger again so had gone straight home, and she wrote to Sandra and to Mary, and then considered the matter closed. Sandra wrote back, enclosing some underwear which had been hanging in the bathroom and which Janet had forgotten, and saying that she was surprised that Janet hadn't bothered to say goodbye to her, but that she had always warned her that actors were the worst possible people to get mixed up with, and was surprised that she, Janet, hadn't taken her advice. Andy and Mary did not reply, but she had hardly expected them to.

On the following Monday she went up to Emerson's and presented herself at the reception desk. The stout commissionaire recognized her and grinned.

' 'Ullo, love. Back again?'

'Could I see Mrs. Landon?' she asked.

'I s'd reckon so. Does t'a want me to ring up?'

'Better. Janet Anderson's my name.'

The commissionaire rang through on the internal phone and asked if Mrs. Landon would see Janet Anderson, and immediately snatched the receiver from his ear and glared at it, muttering something about parrots. He listened again, then put the receiver down and said,

'Aye, you can go up. Know where it is?'

'Is it still Invoicing?' He nodded. 'Then I know, thanks.'

She went up in the lift and walked along the familiar corridors, past the half-frosted doors of various departments, and through the swing doors into Invoicing, and then she paused. For a second she stood unnoticed while everyone carried on with their work or whatever else was occupying their attention, and she had time to notice a new girl sitting at her old desk, and then she was spotted. A squeal of greetings went up and people rushed at her from all sides, wanting to know, all at once, when she had come back, why and for how long. There was Pat and Gloria, Milly from the machine room, Benny and Tony from Costing, even a tight, Nazi sort of smile from Spotty Tomlinson, and Mag and Marj and Mavis, the three typists, jabbering at her like parakeets. Janet smiled a dazed kind of smile and said, 'It's good to be back.'

'Good to be back! You must be going daft,' Gloria said.

'What were it like in London?' little Milly wanted to know. 'We heard you were going out wi' film stars and all-sorts.'

'An' you were gettin' married to some fella on the telly,' Maggie added.

'You don't want to take any notice o' what Vicky Duke says,' Janet said smiling.

'How did you know it were Vicky told us?'

'It sounds like a Vicky story. Hang on, girls, I've got to see Mrs. L. I'll talk to you all later,' she said, and made her escape towards the open door of Mrs. Landon's room. She looked up and smiled as Janet came in.

'Hello, Janet. I heard your voice outside. Come in, sit down. Shut the door behind you, and we'll have a bit of privacy for a few minutes.'

Janet did as she was asked, and sat down, feeling very much at her ease. Her stay in London, short though it had been, had done that much for her. Before she went away she would have sat on the edge of this chair with her hands in her lap – now she sat well back, relaxed, with her legs crossed, not in the least bit self-conscious.

As if she knew what Janet was thinking, Mrs. Landon said, 'London's changed you.'

'Has it?'

'It's given you self-confidence. How was it, anyway? Was it everything you expected?'

Janet thought for a moment, and then said, 'Yes, I think it was. But it wasn't everything I wanted.'

'I think I know what you mean,' the older woman laughed sympathetically. 'Well, I expect you want a job – that would be why you came to see me, wouldn't it?'

'You did say you might be able –'

'Yes, that's right, I did. Well, I expect you noticed that there's someone in your old desk.' Janet nodded. 'And in any case, I think you'd find that rather a dull job after your recent experiences – you were a barmaid, weren't you?'

'How did you – oh, Vicky, I suppose?'

'Yes, she did tell me about her trip to visit you, and said you were getting on well. Of course I was interested. I've often wanted to do a job like that, but I've never quite had the nerve. But look, about this job – the thing is, I can't give you an absolutely firm offer now, but I'll tell you what I had in mind.'

Janet nodded and looked interested. 'I don't expect you will have heard as yet, but Mr. Phillipson, the head buyer, is retiring, and I'm almost certain to get the post. If I do, I shall want an assistant, and I was thinking that you might like to have the job. It would be a more interesting, responsible job than you've had before, with better pay too, of course, and a better future to it.'

'What sort of work would be involved?' Janet asked. It sounded too good to be true.

'More or less everything I'd have to do – you'd be my general assistant. Talking to reps, finding out prices, getting estimates, collating stock reports, making orders, all that sort of thing.'

'It sounds terrific,' Janet said. 'Much better than working that machine.' She nodded towards the door.

'So you would be interested?'

'Yes, of course.'

'Well, I should know some time this week, and if I do get the job, which as I say is almost certain, we'll both start next week, getting into the work of the department before Mr. Phillipson leaves.' Janet nodded. 'So, you give me a ring on, say, Wednesday, and I'll let you know how things stand then. O.K.?'

'Yes, thank you.'

'And, don't say anything about this, will you? Not until it's all settled?'

'No, O.K. But —'

'Yes?' Mrs. Landon raised her eyebrows and smiled as if she knew what was coming.

'Why me?' Janet asked awkwardly. 'I mean, it's almost as if you had this planned. Why do you think I could do the job?'

'I think you're intelligent enough,' Mrs. Landon said. 'I've often watched you out there and thought you were too good to be doing the dull job you did. And then when you decided to go to London, I thought you had the sort of enterprise that was needed for this kind of work. I've been in the running for this job for a long time, you see.'

'Yes, I see. Well, thank you very much, Mrs. Landon, and I'll give you a ring on Wednesday,' Janet said, standing up to go. She hesitated, and then added, 'I think I should enjoy working with you.' And she went out quickly, before the other had time to answer.

She spent the rest of the time until lunch-hour going round the building and visiting all the other departments where she was known, and she sat on desk after desk, smoked cigarette after cigarette, and told an expurgated version of her story so many times over that she almost came to believe it. Then she went up to the canteen to join Vicky for lunch.

Vicky was quite beside herself with pleasure at seeing Janet again.

'Why didn't you let us know you were coming back?' she asked as they shuffled along at the end of the queue. 'We'd have had the works band waiting for you at the station, a police escort, speeches, flowers, the lot.'

'I preferred to sneak back in,' Janet said.

'Like a dog in disgrace. Well, come on then, tell us what

140

you did.'

'Eh?' Janet said vaguely.

'Why did you leave so suddenly? Did you get into trouble with t'police? Are you on the run?' She leaned back and squinted at Janet calculatingly. 'You're not pregnant, are you?'

'Sshh!' Janet said, scandalized. 'If people hear you say that it'll be all over the firm by tea-time. Of course I'm not, what do you take me for?'

'Well tell us then,' Vicky pleaded desperately.

'I just got fed up, and wanted to come home,' Janet said. Vicky turned away, pretending huff.

'Not that I'm interested, o' course.'

'Wait till we sit down,' Janet said quietly, and Vicky gave a huge wink with the whole of the side of her face.

'Curry or rissoles? I think I'll have the curry, just for a change. Change from what I don't know, we only had it on Friday,' Vicky said, picking up a tray and slamming it down on the steel shelf that ran along the front of the counter. Janet followed, noticing that, typically, Vicky had chips and baked beans with her curry and rice. She laughed inwardly, glad to be back, for people just didn't do that in London. She chose rissoles for herself, with chips and peas, and they both took jelly and ice-cream and headed for an empty table in the corner, set rather apart from the others and unpopular because it was just by the door to the toilets.

Vicky unpacked her tray, settled herself in her seat, filled her mouth with the first ravenous forkful, and then said, 'Right, now tell us. Right from the beginning.'

Vicky made a good audience, sitting there with her eyes wide open and her fork automatically filling her mouth whenever it was empty. Moreover, she and Janet were genuinely fond of each other, and her sympathy was real when she said at the end, 'Eh, that were rotten.' She thought for a minute, and then said, 'I think you were brave to come away like that. I think I'd have stayed on and hoped that he'd talk his way out of it – I mean, if I were in love with him as much as you. You're right brave, I mean it.'

'Well, it's all over now, and the sooner I forget him the

141

better. You won't tell anyone, will you, Vick? I don't want it discussed all over the firm.'

'No, all right, I won't. But are you coming back to work here? I heard you were in talking to Mrs. L. t's morning – did she say she'd get you a job?'

'How did you hear about that?'

'I got it off Vera Hopkirk coming out of the toilets, and she got it off Horace, and *he* got it off Tony Smith from Costing, who said he was in Invoicing when you came up.'

'The way things get about in this firm!' Janet laughed.

'Well, when I heard you'd been in, and hadn't even been to see me, I can tell you I was goin' to cross you off my birthday party list. It was a good job for you you turned up when you did. Anyway, did she?'

'Did who, what?' Janet asked, bewildered.

'Mrs. L., say she'd get you a job?'

'Well, I promised her not to tell anyone about it until it was all fixed,' Janet said. Vicky grinned.

'Oh, you mean *you're* the one's going to be her assistant when she gets this new buying job! Congratters! I s'd think everyone in the firm's been after that one. Mrs. L.'s never had so many cups o' tea brought her in all the time she's been here.'

'Now how on earth did you know about that job?' Janet asked, astonished. Vicky screwed up her brow in feigned deep thought.

'Well, let's see now – I had it off Vera Bastowe, and she had it off Tom Waldron's new secretary, and *he* told it *her* when she came for her interview. And he had it off – let me think —'

'No, don't bother, I get the general idea,' Janet said, laughing. 'Well, since you've guessed, that was what she offered me, but still don't say anything until I know if it's going through or not. I'm superstitious.'

'I'm glad it's you,' Vicky said, suddenly serious. 'You always were a cut above us lot, you deserved a better job, and now you've been to London, you're different again.'

'Oh, don't be silly,' Janet began, embarrassed.

'No, really,' Vicky said. 'You've sort of grown up since you went away. The Merry Widow knows that too – trust her for

142

that! That's why she's given you the job.'

'Well I've not got it yet, so just don't talk about it any more. Eat your ice-cream before it gets cold.'

They didn't mention it again, but Janet often thought of what Vicky had said, and she knew that in a way it was true. She was different from the girl who sat staring out of the window last summer at the rain – she was older, and more serious. She had been in love, and she had enjoyed all the frivolous things that you do when you're in love for the first time; and she had been let down; and now she was ready to throw herself into her work fully, and make that her life. It seemed silly to say it when she was still so comparatively young, but she felt that she would never fall in love again; she saw herself as a kind of younger version of Mrs. Landon, a mystery woman, a career woman, set apart from the ordinary round of love and marriage.

CHAPTER FIFTEEN

The phone rang again, and Janet picked it up with a sigh.

'Oh, Miss Anderson, there's a Mr. Tully from Benson and Stavely on the line. He was asking for Mrs. Landon —'

'All right, put him on,' Janet said. There was a pause, a click, and then, 'You're through.'

'Hullo? Mrs. Landon?'

'No, Mrs. Landon's out I'm afraid. This is Miss Anderson, her assistant.'

'Well, it's Tully here, Benson and Stavely – had a message to ring her —'

'Yes, it was about those 9/32 drills. We had a notice from you that they were no longer available, and I've been on to Works, and they say that 1/4 would do.'

'I'm sorry,' said the breathless voice at the other end. 'I thought you would have realized – all our measurements are metric now – that's why we couldn't do the 9/32.'

'All right, well can you do them in 6 mm?' Janet asked wearily.

'Yes, yes, of course. Would that be all right? Do you want to check with your Works?'

'Not necessary, really. If they can lose a thirty-second, then half a millimetre can't make any difference. Send us the usual quantity in 6 mm, will you?'

'Very well, I'll see to that right away. Thank you very much.'

'Thank you. Goodbye.' Janet put the phone down, ran the hair off her forehead with a hand, and then groaned as the phone rang again. She had been virtually on her own in the office all week, for one of Mrs. Landon's children was ill, and she had been going backwards and forwards to the hospital, and when she had been in the office she had been too worried to do much except answer the phone. Added to that, the weather was hot and sultry, the sort of melting, muggy

144

weather that builds up into a tremendous storm, only this had been building up for two weeks and showed no sign of breaking yet.

She picked up the receiver and heard the telephonist's harassed voice, 'Oh, Miss Anderson, there's a Mr. Hopkins in Reception for you, and Carol can't get through on your internal.'

'I told you yesterday it was out of order, and asked you to report it,' Janet said.

'Yes, I know, I did. Do you want to see this Mr. Hopkins?'

'No, tell Carol to say I'm out will you? And don't put any calls through for the next quarter of an hour please – and will you put an outside line on my extension and leave it on until I flash you? I must make some calls.'

'Yes, O.K.,' said the telephonist, and there was a click, a scratching noise, and then the steady burr of an outside line. Thank heaven for that – a bit of peace and quiet! She dialled the speaking clock and left the receiver off the hook – that would ensure that no-one could dial in on that line and get straight through to her. Now for a cup of tea.

She stood up and pulled her skirt away where it had stuck to the back of her legs with perspiration. There were damp patches under her arms, a molten area around her waist, and her hair seemed limp and sticky too. She never had liked August, and this one was no exception. Still, at least this office was on the shaded side of the building for most of the day. At her old desk in Invoicing she would have had the full force of the sun at this time of the afternoon.

She went along to the washroom, washed her hands, splashed her face with cold water, and ran a comb through her hair, and then went to the tea-machine down the corridor and put her money in. She inspected the liquid in the plastic beaker moodily. It was disgusting-looking stuff really, and it didn't taste anything like tea. It didn't taste anything like anything, actually, but she was thirsty, and the only alternative was fizzy orange or coke, both of which made you thirstier, not to mention fat.

She hated August. Last year it had rained all the time. This year it wouldn't rain at all. August never seemed to be able to get it right. She went back into her office. She had her own office now, opening off Mrs. Landon's, and her own telephones, both internal and external – status! It had been a busy year so far, and on the whole a happy one, for the work was interesting, and she liked Mrs. Landon, and if she didn't often get time to stop for coffee or go up to lunch with Vicky and some of the others she probably enjoyed what she was doing instead far more.

Some of the reps who called were good fun, and she had even allowed herself to be taken out for dinner (on expenses, but even so) by one or two of them. She had been out with Tom Waldron a couple of times – that was obligatory for all senior female staff – and she had been out more than a couple of times with one of the junior executives, a nice blond half-German boy called Heinz Uhlman, who was called, predictably, Fifty-seven by Vicky and Co.

Yet it would take more than that to make her forget the blue eyes and the charming boyish smile, the particular arms around her, and the touch of particular lips on her forehead – that greeting that was particularly his. It had seemed easy at first, with the excitement of the new job and the new faces around her, and the widening of her social circle. And when she began to get used to all that, spring had come, bringing with it the revival of outdoor activities, the possibility of Sunday trips, river outings, picnics and so on. So she had found it deceptively easy at first, and sometimes managed to go a whole day without thinking about him.

Then in May she had come home one day to find the new *Radio Times* lying on the top of the television, and on the cover, looking up at her with a burning blue gaze, Roger in his period costume in full colour. The shock of it made her feel faint for a moment, and then she had snatched it up and almost devoured it with her eyes, gazing and gazing as if the picture might speak to her and tell her all the things she wanted to know, how he was, what he had been doing, if he ever thought of her.

Every detail of that face was so well-known to her, and so well-loved. With her eye and with her finger she traced the line of his chin, the slight cleft in it which she had so often

146

touched in the warm, real flesh; his straight nose, the wide, firm mouth with the little grooves at the corners when he smiled; the silky lock of hair that fell forward on to his forehead. Still holding the paper, still gazing at it, unaware that she had not yet taken off her outdoor things, she sat down, remembering everything so clearly and so painfully. Standing beside him in the picture was Stephanie in a bonnet and cloak, looking proud and haughty and very beautiful. She was not right for him, Janet knew quite suddenly. They had been lovers, but she was not right for him. He was in some ways a very ordinary person, with no head for heights, while she was a magnificent hawk, who flew high above everybody else, soaring on powerful wings. She wondered how long it would take poor Roger to find that out.

What did it say about him? *Pride and Prejudice.* Jane Austen's classic story serialized in five parts begins on Tuesday. See page five.' She turned with fumbling fingers to page five, but was disappointed. There was nothing much about him, just a mention that he had the part and that he had been in 'Maple Street' before. Most of the blurb was about the director, and about the scriptwriter who had won an award for his version of *Point Counter Point.* But there was another picture, of the director on location, going over something in the script with Stephanie Sayers, and there, in the background, was Roger, with his hair blowing in the wind, caught in the action of taking the last drag from a cigarette before throwing it down and stamping it out. It was such an ordinary, human action that it had turned her heart over in her, and unlocked the flood gates, and she had sat crying over the picture until her mother couldn't pretend any more that she didn't hear it and had come in from the kitchen to pat her shoulder and make soothing noises.

She had that *Radio Times* still, and took it out now and again to look at the two pictures, and to turn to Tuesday and see his name in the cast list. She had watched every episode, meaning every week not to, and every time being too weak to resist the delicious agony. To see his face again, to hear his voice, even if it was not talking to her, was wonderful, even though to see and hear him declaring love to another woman

147

was torture. All of Emerson's staff had watched those episodes too, though most had been too kind to mention it to Janet, and more than one girl tore the cover off the *Radio Times* of that week and stuck it on her wall or put it away where she kept her treasures.

The serial had won a lot of applause, as Roger predicted, and had been much written about, and Roger had come in for his due share of the bouquets. All the episodes had been repeated on B.B.C. 2 in July, and Janet had found herself once more unable to resist watching it, though now it seemed more strange to her to see him on the television screen than it had before. This time there had been a small picture in the *Radio Times* each week of a scene from that week's episode, and she had torn all of these out and kept them too, ashamed of herself, but helpless – she simply couldn't throw them away.

So it had not been possible for her to forget him, even now, in August, more than half a year since the last time she saw him. She longed to know how he was and what he was doing; she could have written to Andy and asked him, but she was too proud, and it would not have been fair on Andy either. But though she couldn't forget him, she felt more philosophical about it, and she believed that what had happened would have had to happen sooner or later. Actors, especially famous actors, never seemed to have settled relationships – there were very few one could think of who hadn't been divorced at least once, if not several times, and that went for film stars, television stars and musicians too.

Mrs. Landon came in as she was finishing her tea, looking hot and tired, but happy.

'Hello, what's the news?' Janet asked. The other sat down heavily, and smiled.

'He's O.K., he's going to be all right.'

'I'm very glad,' Janet said. 'I was worried about him.'

'I know you were,' Mrs. Landon said. 'You've been very kind, and I'm grateful to you.'

'I haven't done anything,' Janet said awkwardly.

'You've made it possible for me to be with him, by doing my work for me. I think that's a lot, and as I say, I'm grateful, believe me.'

Janet smiled. 'No thanks necessary. I won't say I'm not glad it's Friday, though. You must be glad too – you look nearly melted.'

'I am. It's beastly weather this, but I think it'll break soon, and that has to be for the better.' She looked at Janet closely. 'You're looking fagged. You need a holiday.'

'I never did like August.'

'No, I remember it was August last year that you took off for London.' She stopped suddenly, as if she'd remembered something, and then went on in a different voice. 'Did you ever hear from him?'

Janet looked in surprise at her, and then reflected how things got about the office. 'No,' she said. 'Even if he'd wanted to write, he didn't know where I lived.' Mrs. Landon nodded.

'I expect you were wise,' she said. 'It isn't always easy to be wise until a long time afterwards. I wasn't.'

'What happened to you, then?' Janet asked. She had often wanted to know what happened to Mrs. Landon when she went to London, but had never felt it right to ask.

'Much the same as happened to you – only I wasn't as strong as you. I made sure he knew where to find me when I came back.'

'And did he?'

She nodded. 'That was Mr. Landon. He found me again, and we got married. It didn't last long – only three years – and then he left me, with his two kids, my stepsons, and two new ones to bring up.'

'I thought you were a widow – we all did,' Janet said quietly.

'Yes, well I am. He died four years later.' She was silent, staring into the distance with a little smile on her face. Janet cleared her throat nervously, and said, 'Do you – I suppose you regret it now – letting him know where you were?'

'Regret it? No, I don't think I regret it. Those three years were the happiest years I've ever spent. Some people don't even have that – I might not have if I'd not had him.'

'But you might have married someone else, someone who'd be good to you,' Janet pointed out.

'Yes, perhaps, but then they wouldn't have been Phil, would

they?' Her face was dreamy, and looked very young for a moment, and Janet could see that she must have been quite a stunner when she was younger. Then she came back to the present with a jerk, and looking at Janet said, 'I shouldn't talk that way, should I? You've problems of your own I know – forgive me. Tell you what, you go off home now, make it a nice long weekend. I can finish up here. You deserve a rest.'

'No, really, I —'

'Oh, go on, don't be silly. You've coped alone all week. Now have a few hours on me.'

'All right then, if you're sure. I am feeling a bit tired,' Janet said, but it was sad more than tired. She gave Mrs. Landon the list of people she had to call back, and then picked up her bag and went.

It was only half past four when she got home, and Mum was out somewhere – shopping perhaps for the weekend, for Monday was the Bank Holiday. She got herself a long drink of orange, took off her clothes and put on a cotton nightie to cool off, and then wandered into the sitting room and put on the television, for something to do. She flopped down in a chair and stared at the screen waiting for it to warm up, her mind blank with the heat and tiredness. Slowly the picture came spinning in, and the sound came on, and it was like a slap in the face. There he was, in a white overall and a striped apron, hands on hips, being told off by Mrs. Ogden, the shrill-voiced old harridan in the flowered hat. The tirade came to an end, and she saw his lips part, showing his white teeth, heard his lovely, happy laugh, Mrs. Ogden turned on her heel and flounced out of the shop, and the screen went blank again but for the title, 'Maple Street End of Part One', and the adverts came on.

Janet burst into tears. She had forgotten this series, which evidently was going through yet another repeat, but which she was never at home to see. She was still crying when her mother came home, fifteen minutes later.

'Eh, I'm drenched!' Mum said, coming in from the hall and shaking her head to get the raindrops off. 'What a downpour! Not but we need it right enough —' She stopped short as she saw Janet's tears. 'Eh our Janet, what are you crying for? Not

150

that fella again? There, lass, there, it's all right.'

Janet allowed herself to be comforted, for she had nearly cried herself out anyway, and the programme was over now. Her mother petted her until she was quiet, and then said, 'You come and wash your face, love, and I'll make you a nice cup o' tea. What was it this time? On the telly, was he?' Janet nodded. 'You shouldn't watch it if it upsets you.'

'I didn't know,' Janet explained. 'I just turned it on for something to do, and there he was.'

'Well, never mind, it's all over now. Come on, love, and we'll have a cup o' tea before your father gets in.'

Janet followed her mother into the kitchen, and went to the sink to wash her face. Outside the sky was black and livid, like an old bruise, and it was almost as dark as night as the rain pelted down.

'I didn't think it would come on so soon,' she said as she ran the water.

'What? Oh, t'rain. Aye, I was caught all right. There was no warning at all.'

She busied herself with the tea, and Janet, having washed and dried her face, wandered over to the dresser and fiddled with the cups. Then she noticed a letter addressed to her propped up against the plates.

'Hullo, what's this?' Her mother looked across.

'Oh, aye, that came this morning, after you'd left. T'post-man was late.'

'I don't recognize the writing,' she said, trying hard not to notice that the postmark was London. With a trembling hand she opened it, and smoothed out the single sheet of paper inside.

'Dear Janet,' she read, 'I'm sorry I never replied to that letter of yours but I must admit I was more than a little cross with you for playing the ass. However, that's all past now. Our Mutual Friend, to pass from Austen to Dickens, or from the Sublime to the Ridiculous, sought me out the other day wanting to know if I knew where you were. I intimated I might know if there were good reason. He then poured out his heart to me in a most licenced manner, and said he wanted to write to you. You may hate me for this, but he seemed sincere, if

151

maudlin, so I gave it to him – your address I mean – so you may expect a missive shortly. Yours, Andy.'

Short, and far from sweet, Janet thought, but she could not conceal from herself the excitement she felt, and the violent thudding of her heart. 'You may expect a missive shortly'. What would he write to her about? What else could it be about? It seemed almost too fantastic to be true.

'What is it, love? Not bad news?' Mum asked, concerned by her daughter's peculiar expression.

'It's from a friend in London,' Janet said at last. 'He wants to write to me.'

Her mother looked puzzled. 'You mean he's written to you to ask if he can write to you? That sounds a bit daft to me.'

'No, not him, it's Him, you know – Roger,' she felt embarrassed at saying his name after all this time. 'This friend's written to say Roger wants to write to me.'

'Oh, warnin' you, like? Well, that's friendly anyway. Give you a chance to throw it away wi'out openin' it.'

That hadn't occurred to her, but she knew as soon as Mum said it that she wouldn't do it.

'Oh, no Mum, I'd have to read it.'

'After what he did to you?'

'He didn't do anything to me, Mum. I saw him out with another woman, but I never gave him a chance to explain. He may have had a perfectly good reason.' Mum looked unconvinced. 'Well, he must have some good in him if he wants to write to me after all this time – maybe he wants to explain, or apologize.'

'Took him long enough,' Mum said sourly.

'He wouldn't know where I was. It would be an accident if he met this other friend – they only knew each other by sight.'

Mum softened, and touched Janet's arm.

'I'm only thinking of you, love. I don't want you to be hurt all over again.'

'I know, Mum, and I'll be careful, I promise.'

'Aye, so you say,' Mum said, and she sighed. But she couldn't help noticing the shine of happiness in Janet's face that had been missing since she came back from London, and anything that could put that back couldn't be all bad.

CHAPTER SIXTEEN

The shine had lasted all through Saturday, and Janet had helped her mother with the housework as usual with a most unusual cheerfulness, but after a Saturday night at home, Monday seemed an awfully long way away, a long time to wait until the next post, and when she woke on Sunday the rain was still falling steadily, and she felt dull again.

At least it was cooler, though, and her father was in the best of moods, thinking of his parched garden and burnt brown lawn. He sat in his armchair by the unlit fire, smoking his pipe and reading the Sunday papers, and now and then casting a glance of almost proprietary pride at the teeming window. Janet moved about listlessly, picking up things and putting them down again, and having half-heartedly glanced at two of the papers and annoyed her father by crumpling them, she wandered over to the window and stood there, staring out past the water that streamed down the pane, down the wet, grey street where nothing stirred and there was no sound but the gurgle of the water down the gutter-drains.

She realized that her father and a lot of other people were glad of the rain for their gardens, and she sympathized, but it did stop her going out and doing anything, which might at least have taken her mind off the letter and the wait till Monday and the possibility then of hearing from Roger. She didn't like to speculate what he wanted to write to her about. She could have wished that Andy had been more specific. Poured out his heart, was what he had said – now that could be almost anything: grief, love, remorse. She tried to visualize it, the scene between them, so as to find out what it was most likely that he would say, but she soon found herself cheating and putting words into his mouth, rather than letting them come, so she stopped and stared out of the window again.

Someone was coming along the street. They must be mad, going out like that with only a jacket on. Looked as though he didn't know where he was going, too, walking slowly, looking at the numbers on the houses. Her heart began to beat faster. Surely it couldn't be —? The rain was pelting so hard it made a fine mist around the solitary wet figure, but could she mistake the shape, the dark hair, the way of walking. He was crossing the road, coming towards the house. She left the window and walked quietly, not to arouse her father, out of the front room, across the hall to the front door, and as a figure shadowed the frosted panel at the top she opened it.

He stood there, his hand raised to press the bell, stopped in the middle of the movement. She was reminded of that other time he had come to her out of the rain, to tell her about his great new part, but he was wetter now, far wetter. His jacket was dark with rain, his hair flat to his head with it, his trousers soaked and mud-spattered, his shoes cardboardy with it. Water ran across his face, and gathered in big shining drops on his eyelashes and dripped off the end of his nose. They looked at each other for a long minute, without smiling, and then he said,

'Jan, I want to talk to you.'

She looked over her shoulder into the house, but he shook his head.

'Alone. Please Janet.' She hesitated for a moment, and then shrugged and, feeling rather like a swimmer pushing off, she stepped out into the rain with him and closed the door. He scarcely seemed to notice it, but she was struck at first by how cold the rain was as it penetrated her thin dress to her skin. They walked along the street and she turned the corner and walked in the general direction of the park; though she was not really aware of it, and Roger followed her. He didn't seem particularly anxious to talk, so she said at last, 'Andy wrote and said you'd asked for my address to write to me.'

Roger nodded, looking as though he was good for another ten minutes' silence, and then quite suddenly he stopped and took her hand and turned her to face him, and began to speak, just where he stood on the corner of Molton Street and Bears Lane.

'Janet, I know I behaved like an idiot. I can see it now, though at the time I didn't realize it. You know what was wrong with me, don't you? Just sheer big-headedness. I thought I was the greatest thing since sliced bread, and I made a complete fool of myself, and I was rotten to you. I really was a pig, Jan, and I want to apologize. I was going to write and say how sorry I was, but then I realized that that wouldn't be good enough – it would almost be like another insult, so I got the train instead to come and see you and tell you myself. I'm sorry, Jan, really sorry.'

He stopped, looking pathetic in the rain, and, to do him credit, really sorry. She didn't know what to say, but it wasn't really necessary – having wound himself up he could carry on without prompts.

'I didn't mean to hurt you, Jan, and I didn't realize that I was. I got big-headed, and thought that I could take Stephanie out on the side like a gay dog and that you'd never find out. I convinced myself that it didn't matter, that everyone did it, that men weren't expected to keep to one girl only – all the usual sort of rubbish. You know how men go on when they're like that.' She nodded, but he didn't seem to see her. 'And I believed it all. Then when you disappeared, I convinced myself that I didn't care about that either, and I just went on like before only worse, missing you like hell and pretending to myself that I didn't.'

She saw his eyes change focus, and knew that now he was looking at her. His voice became softer, more like his own voice and less like an actor's.

'So I've come to say I'm sorry, and ask you to forgive me.'

'I forgive you,' she said. There didn't seem to be much else she could say. Now there was more water than just rain on her face, and she could feel the heat of the drops that ran down from her eyes. Roger's face came very close to hers, and for a moment she saw it blurred, and then she closed her eyes, for his mouth was on hers and she was kissing him, their two faces pressed together in the streaming water, and there was the metallic taste of the rain in her mouth and the salt taste of tears.

They kissed and kissed and kissed again, and she heard, hardly believing it, Roger saying, 'I love you, Jan, I love you.' He said a lot of other things, mostly incoherent, before the

155

man outside whose front-room window they were standing came to his front door and told them to go away.

'Disgusting! Indecent! Go away before I call the police!' he shouted. The rain seemed to come down even harder, and they both looked up at the sky, and laughed. An old woman appeared behind the man and said 'Loonies, that's what they are, loonies got out o' somewhere,' and Roger and Janet joined hands and started to run down the street, still laughing.

They got to the main road, and Roger pulled her after him into a bus shelter, and they sat down on the bench laughing and panting.

'They must have thought we were potty,' Janet said when she got her breath back.

'We are,' Roger said. 'Crazy in love,' and he began to kiss her again. She pushed him back.

'It's all right for you, I've got to live here. You can't do that sort of thing in this town, you know – this isn't London.'

'I know – kiss me.'

'Oh no, you've got a lot more explaining to do yet,' Janet said firmly, and he gave a huge sigh, but his eyes were laughing. 'Now, if you really felt that way about me, why did it take you so long to find me?'

'I did try,' he said. 'As soon as I came to my senses I went round to your flat to ask Sandra your address, but she'd left, and the person who'd taken the flat said there wasn't a forwarding address. I thought maybe they were just being careful, so I wrote to her at the flat and put 'please forward' on the envelope, but nothing ever came of it. I asked at the pub, but they either didn't know or wouldn't tell me – probably the latter – and after that my inventiveness ran out.'

'All right, but you said "when you came to your senses" – when was that?'

'You do sound strict. Just like my mother. I can't remember exactly when it was but I suppose it was about a month after you left. Steve gave me a good dressing down one day and told me I should be ashamed of myself, and he said that you were the best thing that ever happened to me – which was true – and the only thing that had kept me even a tolerable person.'

'I always thought Steve didn't like me.'

156

'Oh, that's just his way. He thought the world of you. Anyway, he told me what a bunch of crap I was, and Stephanie seconded that opinion, and I began to see the light.'

Janet thought she could read between the lines there – she saw the scenes like a film passing in front of her eyes, Stephanie getting tired of him and throwing him over, him moping around the flat, Steve losing his temper, and then Roger beginning to feel lonely and missing her. It wasn't as flattering as the picture Roger painted for her, but did it really matter?

'So how did you finally get on to Andy?' she said.

'I ran into him by accident – I didn't know him very well, of course, and then I remembered that you had used to be pally with him, so I hung around the Centre until he came out, and then asked him if he knew your address. He took some persuading, I can tell you.'

The rain was beginning to slacken, and Janet felt that she must get back home, for neither of her parents knew where she was, and she hadn't even taken her coat.

'I'll have to get back,' she said. Roger stood up immediately, and took her hand, preparing to duck out into the rain.

'I can come and meet them, can't I?' She looked at him in surprise, and doubt, and seeing her expression he stopped too. 'What's the matter? You aren't ashamed of me, are you? Oh, I see – you've painted the picture so black I'd be seen off with a shotgun, is that it?'

'No, not at all,' she denied hastily. 'I didn't tell them much about you at all, but when I got Andy's letter I tried to put your stock up a bit.'

'Well then, what's the matter?'

'I was wondering – I mean, why do you want to see them?'

'Well, it is customary, when you're going to get married, to meet your future in-laws.' Roger said it with heavy irony, and she looked at him with continued doubt.

'It's also customary to ask your future wife if she'll *be* your future wife,' she said.

'But I thought that was all settled! You do love me, don't you?'

'Yes, of course I do.'

157

'Then what's the problem?' He seemed genuinely distressed.

'Roger, don't be hurt, but – I don't think I could marry an actor. I'd never know if you were going to catch the same sickness again – and it is a sickness you know. It would be so easy, you know.'

Still standing in the rain, he looked at her with an expression of softly quizzical humour, a bit like a spaniel trying to share the joke.

'Thank you, darling, for being so frank with me. But you needn't worry – I'm not going to be an actor any more. I haven't had any more work since that big part; no-one's interested. I was just a flash in the pan.' He was probably not aware of the bitterness in his voice when he said that, but it came over clearly enough to Janet.

'But what will you do then?'

'I'll get a job, like anyone else. I'll be able to find something to do all right, don't worry. I won't let you down.'

They began to walk down the road, and Janet's face was pulled into a worried frown. Strangely enough she hadn't expected him to say he would give up acting, and it left her with rather a profound problem to solve. She thought aloud.

'Now I come to think of it, I don't know that that would be any good anyway. I mean, you are an actor from choice, it's your chosen career, and if you gave it up there would always be that unfulfilled desire in you to act. It might make you resent me. It would almost certainly make you unhappy. How can I ask you to give up acting? I don't really think I can.'

Roger looked at her now in absolute misery; the spaniel was now a beaten one.

'That means that you won't marry me at all. That you don't love me. You won't forgive me.'

The rain stopped at last, and there was a quietness over everything, except for the soft drip-drip of the soaking wet, steaming world. Janet stared at him, and tried to imagine life without him again, and she knew it was no good. She remembered, as she had before at a cross-roads in her life, Mrs. Landon; remembered her saying, 'No, I don't regret it.' It occurred to her that what she had called a sickness was a part

158

of Roger himself, not of his way of life, and that whatever job he did for a living, it was just as likely to strike. And if it did, they would either live through it, and love each other again, or they would part. She couldn't know which it would be, and she wouldn't really want to know. However long it was, that was her destiny, and she had to live by it.

She took Roger's hand, and looked up into his glorious face with all the trust and love in her nature.

'Rodge, I've no right to tell you what to do with your life. I do love you, and I'll marry you, whatever you want to do. If you want to give up acting, I don't mind, but if you want to go on with it, I'll be behind you all the way.'

He looked down at her, smiling.

'My darling, with you as my wife, there's only one way I can go, and that's to the top.'

They fell in side by side and began walking back, through a world that suddenly glittered with a million raindrops reflecting the new August sun.